ЧтениЯReadings

Chtenia: Readings from Russia

a themed journal
of fiction, non-fiction, poetry,
photography and miscellany

ISSN 1939-7240 • Volume 8, Number 3 • Issue 27

Chtenia is a quarterly journal of readings from Russia, including fiction, non-fiction, memoirs, humor, poetry and photography. Opinions expressed are those of the authors and do not necessarily reflect the views of the staff, management or publisher of *Chtenia.*

Publisher: Paul E. Richardson
Managing Editor: Olga Kuzmina
Issue Curator: Boris Dralyuk

Chtenia Subscription rates (1 year): US $35, Outside US $43. All prices are in U.S. dollars. Back issues: when available: $10 (shipping and handling additional). Newsstand: $10 per issue. • To notify us of a change of address, see the subscription address below. To ensure that you do not miss any issues, please notify us 4-6 weeks in advance of any move or address change. Periodical postage paid at Montpelier, VT and at additional mailing offices (USPS 024-769).

Publications Mail Agreement No. 40649170. Return undeliverable Canadian Address to: Station A, PO Box 54, Windsor, ON N9A 6J5. Email: orders@russianlife.com

POSTMASTER: Please send change of address and subscription applications to:
RIS Publications, PO Box 567, Montpelier, VT 05601-0567
orders@russianlife.com
Ph. 802-234-1956 • Fax: 802-254-8511
www.chtenia.com

27

The War to End All

ЧтениЯReadings

Vol. 8, No. 3 • Summer 2014 • Issue 27

Contents

Russia's Great War
Boris Dralyuk

It would be inaccurate to say that the First World War – the conflict George F. Kennan called the "seminal evil of the twentieth century" – is Russia's forgotten war, eclipsed by the internal conflagration of the Revolution and its aftermath.[1] Russia's participation in the Great War wasn't eclipsed by the birth pangs of the Soviet Union. Instead, it was inscribed in the Soviet Union's origin story to such a degree that today, in hindsight, one can hardly see it in isolation. From the 1920s onward, Russian authors who wrote about the First World War both in the Soviet Union and in emigration tended to treat it as part of a larger story, rather than as a story in itself.

Nikolai Tikhonov (1896-1979), one of the Soviet poets most firmly associated with the First World War, is a fine example of this phenomenon. In his highly praised and enormously popular collections *The Horde* (*Орда*, 1922) and *Mead* (*Брага*, 1922), he speaks for a generation that came of age with the help of "Fire, the rope, the bullet, and the axe." His poems brim with vivid images of battle, nights on watch, and other wartime

---

1. Karen Petrone's recent study *The Great War in Russian Memory* (Bloomington: Indiana UP, 2011) analyzes the conflict's legacies in Russian and Soviet culture.

scenes. What is remarkable, however, is the difficulty one has in "placing" the experience they describe. In some cases, it is simply impossible to tell whether Tikhonov is drawing on his time as a Hussar in the Imperial Army during the First World War, or on his service as a Red Army man during the Civil War. It may be precisely this quality that resonated with Tikhonov's readers – the sense that he'd captured the long, torturous process of tempering through which his steely generation had passed. This process may have encompassed discrete wars, but, for those on the ground, it felt like one fiery campaign. "They ought to make nails out of these folks," one of Tikhonov's most famous ballads concludes. "There'd be no tougher nails in all the world."

Soviet prose authors who had fought in the Great War also depicted their service as a formative experience, a period of ideological awakening. The Russian-Jewish author Kirill Levin (1898-1980), who had been a prisoner in Austro-Hungarian and German P.O.W. camps, wrote memoirs and "documentary" fiction presenting the Great War as an imperialist conflict, in which the soldiers on both sides were merely pawns who had more in common with one another than with their own commanders. This resonated with the views expressed in West European anti-war classics like Henri Barbusse's *Under Fire: The Story of a Squad* (1916), Robert Graves's *Good-Bye to All That* (1929), and Erich Maria Remarque's *All Quiet on the Western Front* (1929). It's no surprise, then, that Levin's story of a mutiny led by Austrian and Russian troops, "The Wild Battalion," appeared in an international collection of pacifist writing titled *We Did Not Fight* (1935), edited by the British poet Julian Bell. It's also no surprise that, as Karen Petrone demonstrates in *The Great War in Russian Memory*, this pacifist, internationalist stance became less and less acceptable as the Soviet Union commenced its lurch toward war with Germany in the 1930s.[2]

---

2. See Petrone, chs. 6 and 7.

If for Tikhonov and other Soviet authors of his generation the Great War represented the beginning of a new era, for those set adrift by the Revolution it marked the beginning of the end. Many émigrés, both external and internal, came to associate the year 1913 with the last flowering of pre-Revolutionary culture. In her epic *Poem Without a Hero* (*Поэма без героя*, 1940-1965), Anna Akhmatova (1889-1966) casts a glance back at the vanished St. Petersburg of the last year before the war, while a powerful 1926 lyric by Georgy Ivanov (1894-1958) begins:

In 1913, not yet comprehending
what would befall us, what was drawing near,
we raised our glasses of champagne and
cheerfully greeted – the New Year.

The sense of a flowering cut off too suddenly and too soon is captured affectingly in Ivan Bunin's (1870-1953) short story "The Cold Fall" (1944), in which an émigré woman describes the last evening she spent with her beloved thirty years earlier, in 1914, before his departure for the front. Mikhail Zoshchenko's (1895-1958) novella *Before Sunrise*, written in the 1930s and 1940s, but not published until 1968, and then only abroad, presents an even more subtle and psychologically penetrating portrait of the Great War's role in the development and expression of this nominally Soviet author's personality.

All the works discussed so far are retrospective; inevitably, they all take the long view, encompassing both the Great War and what came after. Brief prose sketches, journalism, and, above all, poems composed as the conflict unfolded, give us a clearer sense of the war's immediate impact, and of the rifts it caused – and exposed – in Russian society.[3]

3. This volume includes both patriotic texts, and those critical of unbridled nationalism and militarism. For an overview of Russian patriotism during the Great War, see Hubertus F. Jahn, *Patriotic Culture in Russia During World War I* (Ithaca, NY: Cornell UP, 1995).

The Great War occurred during the last half-decade of the so-called Silver Age of Russian poetry, and most of the important poets of the period expressed their thoughts on and impressions of the conflict in lyric verse. As the scholar Ben Hellman has shown, the Symbolists – who had virtually monopolized the Russian poetic scene from the 1890s to 1910, and who still represented the poetic "establishment" in 1914-1917 – greeted the war in a wide variety of ways.[4] Their reactions ranged from Fyodor Sologub's (1863-1927) neo-Slavophilic patriotism, exemplified by the faux-naïf jingoism of "A Wife to a Reservist;" to Zinaida Gippius's (1869-1945) and Maximilian Voloshin's (1877-1932) conscientious refusal to celebrate bloodshed in the former's "Quiet" and "Without Justification" and the latter's "Newspapers;" and to Alexander Blok's (1880-1921) reconciliation with the frightening but irrepressible march of history in "The Petrograd Sky..."

The younger, post-Symbolist poets were no less varied in their reactions. To get a sense of the internal divisions among the Acmeists, one need only compare the dire, apocalyptic vision of Akhmatova's "In Memoriam, July 19, 1914," commemorating the declaration of war, to the unabashed idealism, stylized imagery, and elevated tone of her husband Nikolai Gumilyov's (1886-1921) "War," drawn from his collection *The Quiver* (*Колчан*, 1916). Sergei Gorodetsky's (1884-1967) patriotic "Knight of the Air" is, appropriately enough, even loftier in tone than Gumilyov's poem; it sings the praises of Pyotr Nesterov, a pioneering Russian aviator who sacrificed his life to bring down an Austrian plane on August 26, 1914. Gumilyov was a cavalry officer in the Imperial Army and remained loyal to the monarchist cause, but his heroic poems clearly left their mark on Tikhonov, his poetic disciple, who wound up on the other end of the ideological spectrum.

The programmatically fractious Futurists were, as one might imagine, more divided yet. The dandified Ego-Futurist Igor Severyanin's (1887-1941) ironic promise in "My Response" to lead his audience to Berlin – but only if the need should arise – demonstrates a woeful misapprehension of the

4. Ben Hellman, *Poets of Hope and Despair: The Russian Symbolists in War and Revolution (1914-1918)* (Helsinki: Institute for Russian and East European Studies, 1995).

severity of the crisis. The Cubo-Futurist Vladimir Mayakovsky (1893-1930) initially saw the outbreak of war as the arrival of a subject grand enough for his extraordinary poetic gifts, but was soon repelled by its horrors; his "War's Declared" and "Mama and the Evening Killed by the Germans" chart his rapid disenchantment. Mayakovsky, who would take up the role of the Bolshevik's tribune after the Revolution, was instrumental in establishing the First World War as part of a larger ideological narrative. As he and the post-Revolutionary Futurists of the "Left Front of Art" wrote in 1922, contextualizing his major long poem *A Cloud in Trousers* (*Облако в штанах*, 1915), "The war wished to see tomorrow's revolution" ("What Is LEF Fighting For?").

In addition to poems written between 1914 and 1917, we also include an excerpt from Ilya Ehrenburg's (1891-1967) *The Face of War* (*Лик войны*, 1920), which collected his frontline reporting from France and constituted a powerful indictment of the horrors of war, as well as Leonid Andreyev's (1871-1919) "Wounded Soldier," which bares the hypocrisy of Russia's systemic anti-Semitism. Perhaps the most powerful piece of prose in the volume is Nadezhda Teffi's (1872-1952) characteristically perceptive "Ya-vdokha," which vividly captures the inanity, the utter senselessness of the conflict on a humble but profoundly tragic scale.

The Contributors

ANNA AKHMATOVA (pseudonym of Anna Andreyevna Gorenko, 1889-1966) is one of Russia's most acclaimed poets. The daughter of a naval engineer, she became a member of the Acmeist group of poets, led by her future husband Nikolai Gumilyov, when she was 21. She married Gumilyov in 1910 and they had one son, Lev. They were divorced in 1918. After Gumilyov was executed in 1921 for antirevolutionary activities, Akhmatova entered a period of almost complete poetic silence until 1940. When her son was exiled to Siberia, she attempted to help him by penning a poem eulogizing Stalin: *Поема без героя* (*Poem Without a Hero*, 1963). It was begun in Leningrad in 1940 and revised for over 20 years. One of her finest works, *Реквием* (*Requiem*, 1963) is a poem-cycle that was a literary monument to the victims of Stalin's Terror.

LEONID NIKOLAIEVICH ANDREYEV (1871-1919) was one of the finest writers of Russia's Silver Age. The author of many tragic works distinguished by their hopelessness and negative views on the nature of man and his existence, Andreyev's earlier works focused on social contradictions in Russian society. Yet, with time, his books became increasingly more symbolic and filled with existential despair. Perhaps it is not surprising, therefore, that Andreyev's life had its fill of tragedy. His initial enthusiasm for revolutionary ideas was soon replaced by a total rejection of the revolution. He died in emigration, in Finland, despairing at what was unfolding in Russia.

12   **ALEXANDER BLOK** (1880-1921) was one of the greatest Russian poets of the Silver Age of Russian literature (1890-1920). A leader of the Symbolist movement, he invented a new poetic language in his poems *Retribution* (1910-1919) and *The Twelve* (1918).

ROBERT BOWIE is professor emeritus of Russian at Miami University of Ohio. His translations of Ivan Bunin have been collected in *Night of Denial: Stories and Novellas* (Northwestern University Press, 2006).

IVAN BUNIN (1870-1953) was Russia's first Nobel Laureate for literature (1933). His writing is richly textured and evocative of a more prosaic, humane, prerevolutionary era. A friend of Anton Chekhov, Bunin worked for a time in Kharkov as a government clerk and editor, did translations from English, and wrote his short stories, by the turn of the century becoming recognized as one of Russia's greatest living writers. He lived in emigration from 1919 until his death in Paris in 1953.

BORIS DRALYUK holds a Ph.D. in Slavic Languages and Literatures from University of California, Los Angeles. His work has appeared in a variety of journals, including *The New Yorker*, *The Times Literary Supplement*, and *World Literature Today*. He has translated and co-translated several volumes of poetry and prose from Russian and Polish and is co-editor, with Robert Chandler and Irina Mashinski, of the forthcoming *Penguin Book of Russian Poetry* (Penguin Classics, 2015). His translation of Isaac Babel's *Red Cavalry* is forthcoming from Pushkin Press in November 2014. He received first prize in the 2011 Compass Translation Award competition and, with Irina Mashinski, first prize in the 2012 Joseph Brodsky / Stephen Spender Translation Prize competition.

ILYA EHRENBURG (1891-1967), born to a Jewish family in Kiev, became involved in the Bolshevik movement as early as 1905, in the wake of the first Russian Revolution. After his arrest and brief imprisonment by the Tsarist Okhrana in 1908, he was exiled to Paris, where he continued his political work and began his literary career as a poet and journalist in Montparnasse. Upon returning to Russia after the October Revolution, he grew temporarily disillusioned with the Bolshevik cause, put off by the violence he saw around him. He eventually reconciled with the regime, but preferred to spend his time abroad as a "cultural ambassador." His lasting literary contributions are the pessimistic satirical novels he wrote in the early

1920s, most notably *The Extraordinary Adventures of Julia Jurenito and his Disciples* (1922). He will also be remembered for his work – alongside Vasily Grossman and members of the Jewish Anti-Fascist Committee – on the *Black Book*, one of the first documents to chronicle the horrors of the Holocaust, and for his novel *The Thaw* (1954), which lent its name to the period of liberalization that followed Stalin's death.

SERGEI GORODETSKY (1884-1967) began his career as a Symbolist poet, working with themes drawn from Slavic folklore. In 1911 he rejected the mysticism of the Symbolists and, together with Nikolai Gumilyov, founded the Guild of Poets and the Acmeist movement. After the Revolution and Gumilyov's arrest and execution, Gorodetsky repudiated his former friend and became a Soviet poet.

ZINAIDA GIPPIUS (1869-1945) was a writer, poet and religious thinker, and one of the most influential Russian women of her age. With her husband, Dmitry Merezhkovsky, she founded the Symbolist movement. While she welcomed the February 1917 revolution, she was one of the first artists to publicly denounce the Bolshevik Revolution. She and her husband emigrated to Europe in 1919.

NIKOLAI GUMILYOV (1886-1921) was a leading poet of the Silver Age of Russian literature (1890-1920). A founder of the Acmeist movement, he was Anna Akhmatova's first husband and the father of historian Lev Gumilyov. He traveled extensively around the world, including on an expedition in Africa. In 1921 he was shot by the Bolsheviks on trumped up conspiracy charges.

JUDITH HEMSCHEMEYER is a retired professor of English who has been writing about and translating Russian poetry for several decades. Her *Complete Poems of Anna Akhmatova* (Zephyr Press, 1990) is widely considered the finest English translation of the great poet's works.

ANNE MARIE JACKSON lived in both Russia and Moldova in the 1990s. In Moldova, she was once shot dead by Chechen rebels in a Russian film. She studied translation at University College London and has since translated works by Maxim Osipov, Alexei Nikitin and Nadezhda Teffi, among others. She is the editor of *Subtly Worded and Other Stories by Teffi*, published by Pushkin Press in 2014.

14   **VALENTIN PETROVICH KATAYEV** (1897-1986) was a novelist and playwright. He showed remarkable political savvy, penning both works that satirized Soviet bureaucracy and that glorified Soviet achievements throughout a career that was both long and prolific. He is credited with suggesting the idea of *The Twelve Chairs* (1927) to his brother Yevgeny Petrov and Ilya Ilf, the price of which was that all editions of the book had to be dedicated to him.

GARY KERN earned his Ph.D. in Russian literature from Princeton University in 1969 and has taught Russian and world literature at the University of Rochester, the University of California, Riverside, and the University of Southern California. He has translated eight books from Russian, including *Before Sunrise* by Mikhail Zoshchenko (Ardis, 1974), *The Education of a True Believer* by Lev Kopelev (Harper & Row, 1980) and *This I Cannot Forget: The Memoirs of Nikolai Bukharin's Widow* by Anna Larina (Norton, 1993). He is also the author of the critically acclaimed study *The Kravchenko Case* (Enigma Books, 2007), and *A Death in Washington: Walter G. Krivitksy and the Stalin Terror* (Enigma Books, 2003). He also wrote the play *The Mad Kokoschka* (1986), the memoirs *Misfortune* (1997), and *Letters From Dwight* (1998), all published by Xenos Books. His novel, *The Last Snow Leopard* (Ghost Dance, 1996), will soon be available from Xenos.

KIRILL LEVIN (1892-1980) was a Soviet Jewish author who fought in the First World War and was held prisoner at both Austro-Hungarian and German POW camps. His experiences at the front and in captivity provided material for a series of popular memoirs and "documentary novels" published in the 1920s and 1930s.

VLADIMIR MAYAKOVSKY (1893-1930) has always sparked a wide range of emotions and opinions. He was reviled by many for his support of the Bolshevik Revolution. Yet, by the end of the 1920s, the numbing effects of the system he had so welcomed eventually led to his suicide. For the next few years, his work was officially censored. Then, on Stalin's personal decision, Mayakovsky was transformed into the "greatest Soviet poet." This led later generations to perceive him as a shill for the communist regime. But even as early as the late 1950s, an alternative view of him developed – as a free-spirited rebel – spurred by young poets who would gather at his monument in Moscow and demonstratively read his poetry.

JAMES MCGAVRAN has taught Russian language and culture courses at Kenyon College, St. Olaf College, and Rutgers University, and he begins work as a lecturer in Russian at the University of Pennsylvania in the fall of 2014. His book of annotated translations of the poet Vladimir Mayakovsky, *Selected Poems*, is now available from Northwestern University Press, and he has also published articles and translations in *Slavonica, Modern Poetry in Translation*, and *Slavic and East European Journal.*

DORIAN ROTTENBERG was a noted translator of Russian literature, specializing in the translation of poetry (particularly Mayakovsky) and children's books.

IGOR SEVERYANIN (pseudonym of Igor Lotaryov, 1887-1941), the leader of the so-called Ego-Futurists, was one of the most popular and controversial poets of the Silver Age (1890-1920). He struck a provocative dandified pose both in his life and his work, singing the praises of "pineapples in champagne" and "lilac ice-cream" in verse brimming with foreign borrowings and neologisms. He fled Russia to Estonia in 1917, where he continued to write poetry, but now of a much more subdued nature. He died of a heart attack in Tallinn in 1941.

NINA SHEVCHUK-MURRAY was born and raised in L'viv. She holds degrees in English linguistics and Creative Writing and translates both poetry and prose from the Russian and Ukrainian languages. Her translations and original poetry have been published in a number of literary magazines. With Ladette Randolph, she co-edited the anthology of Nebraska non-fiction *The Big Empty* (U of NE Press, 2007). She has translated Peter Aleshkovsky's novel *Fish: A History of One Migration* (short-listed for the Rossica Translation Prize), Oksana Zabuzhko's *Museum of Abandoned Secrets* and Aleshkovsky's *Stargorod.*

EUGENIA SOKOLSKAYA came to the United States from Russia when she was four. In addition to a normal public-school education, she also received extensive instruction in Russian literature, film, and history from her parents. She is a graduate of Swarthmore College and a freelance translator. In 2011, she was short-listed for the Rossica Young Translators Award.

FYODOR SOLOGUB (pseudonym of Fyodor Kuzmich Teternikov, 1863-1927) was one of the most important poets of the Silver Age in Russian literature (1890-1920). A Symbolist, he authored a great number of poems, and his best-known novel was *The Petty Demon* (1907). He was one of the first Russian authors to introduce the morbid, pessimistic elements characteristic of *fin de siècle* literature into his prose; readers were both attracted and repulsed by his mesmerizing ideas of death and evil.

NADEZHDA TEFFI (pseudonym of Nadezhda Lokhvitskaya, 1872-1952) was a literary superstar in pre-revolutionary Russia, whose witty, pointed, but unoffensive stories about the absurdities of life were memorized and quoted as soon as they were published, and whose legions of fans included all echelons of Russian society. In emigration she wrote about the many incongruities she observed in the Russian émigré community; these stories were pirated in Russia, where they were used to advance the thesis that the Russian émigrés were rotting away due to the emptiness and hopelessness of their lives. In response, Teffi wrote a public letter insisting that Soviets cease and desist; they did, but they also did not publish any of her stories at all for nearly fifty years.

NIKOLAI TIKHONOV (1896-1979) was born to petty tradesmen descended from serfs. Trained as a clerk, he volunteered for the army at the outbreak of WWI and served in the hussars, then served in the Red Army from 1918 to 1922. Devoting himself almost exclusively to writing and travel after 1922, Tikhonov became a founding member of the Serapion Brothers literary group, and was chair of the Union of Writers from 1944-46, a position from which he was dismissed by Stalin for being too tolerant of Zoshchenko and Akhmatova. He nonetheless remained influential in literary circles until his death.

CAPTAIN DONALD C. THOMPSON (1884-1947) was an iconic, adventure-seeking war photographer born in Topeka, Kansas. He was the first American photographer at Verdun, and war journalist Edward Powell said of him that he had "more chilled-steel nerve than any man I know." Thompson repeatedly risked his life to capture the war on still and movie film, before returning to the US to share his experiences and images in public lectures, bringing the horrors of the war to US audiences. He supplied most of the footage for a 1915 film, *With the Russians at the Front.*, and *War as it Really Is* (1916) among others. In late 1916 Thompson was sent to Petrograd with Florence Harper to cover the Russian side of the war for *Leslie's Weekly* when the February Revolution broke out. His photographs from 1917 are a stark and rich documentary of events. The photos in this issue are taken from his 1918 book covering that period, *Blood-Stained Russia*.

MAXIMILIAN VOLOSHIN (1877-1932) was a Symbolist poet, painter, critic and translator. His home in the Crimea was a refuge for most of the Silver Age's brightest literary and artistic talents. And yet, he is little known outside Russia. After his death, his residence in Crimea – Koktebel – became a famous summer resort for writers.

AVRAHM YARMOLINSKY (1890-1975) was born in what is now Ukraine and emigrated to the United States in 1913. He graduated from the City College of New York and earned his Ph.D. at Columbia University, later teaching Russian language and literature at both institutions, as well as heading the Slavonic Division of the New York Public Library. He wrote extensively on Russian literature and intellectual history, and translated many classics. He was the husband of poet Babette Deutsch, with whom he co-translated and co-edited anthologies of Russian and German poetry.

MIKHAIL ZOSHCHENKO (1895-1958) was a remarkable writer, especially popular in the 1920s for his satirical stories that skewered Soviet reality. Zoshchenko sought to conceptualize what was new and positive in Soviet life, seeking a completely new language to describe it, one that was simple and "naked," in compact sentences that were, in his words, "accessible to the poor." In 1946, along with Anna Akhmatova and others, he was subjected to severe official criticism. After Stalin's death, he refused to acknowledge his guilt and, despite the Khrushchevian Thaw, was subjected to further persecution, which contributed to years of ill health prior to his death.

Памяти 19 июля 1914 года
Анна Ахматова

Мы на сто лет состарились, и это
Тогда случилось в час один:
Короткое уже кончалось лето,
Дымилось тело вспаханных равнин.

Вдруг запестрела тихая дорога,
Плач полетел, серебряно звеня.
Закрыв лицо, я умоляла Бога
До первой битвы умертвить меня.

Из памяти, как груз отныне лишний,
Исчезли тени песен и страстей.
Ей – опустевшей – приказал Всевышний
Стать страшной книгой грозовых вестей.

18 июля 1916, Слепнево

In Memoriam, July 19, 1914
Anna Akhmatova

We aged a hundred years, and this
Happened in a single hour:
The short summer had already died,
The body of the ploughed plains smoked.

Suddenly the quiet road burst into color,
A lament flew up, ringing, silver...
Covering my face, I implored God
Before the first battle to strike me dead.

Like a burden henceforth unnecessary,
The shadows of passion and songs vanished from my memory.
The Most High ordered it – emptied –
To become a grim book of calamity.

18 July 1916, Slepnevo
Translation by Judith Hemschemeyer

Июль 1914

Анна Ахматова

I

Пахнет гарью. Четыре недели
Торф сухой по болотам горит.
Даже птицы сегодня не пели,
И осина уже не дрожит.

Стало солнце немилостью Божьей,
Дождик с Пасхи полей не кропил.
Приходил одноногий прохожий
И один на дворе говорил:

«Сроки страшные близятся. Скоро
Станет тесно от свежих могил.
Ждите глада, и труса, и мора,
И затменья небесных светил.

Только нашей земли не разделит
На потеху себе супостат:
Богородица белый расстелет
Над скорбями великими плат».

II

Можжевельника запах сладкий
От горящих лесов летит.
Над ребятами стонут солдатки,
Вдовий плач по деревне звенит.

Не напрасно молебны служились,
О дожде тосковала земля:
Красной влагой тепло окропились
Затоптанные поля.

Низко, низко небо пустое,
И голос молящего тих:
«Ранят тело твое пресвятое,
Мечут жребий о ризах твоих».

20 июля 1914
Слепнево

July 1914
Anna Akhmatova

1

It smells of burning. For four weeks
The dry peat bog has been burning.
The birds have not even sung today,
And the aspen has stopped quaking.

The sun has become God's displeasure,
Rain has not sprinkled the fields since Easter.
A one-legged stranger came along
And all alone in the courtyard he said:

"Fearful times are drawing near. Soon
Fresh graves will be everywhere.
There will be famine, earthquakes, widespread death,
And the eclipse of the sun and the moon.

But the enemy will not divide
Our land at will, for himself:
The Mother of God will spread her white mantle
Over this enormous grief."

2

The sweet smell of juniper
Flies from the burning woods.
Soldiers' wives are wailing for the boys,
The widow's lament keens over the countryside.

The public prayers were not in vain,
The earth was yearning for rain!
Warm red liquid sprinkled
The trampled fields.

Low, low hangs the empty sky
And a praying voice quietly intones:
"They are wounding your sacred body,
They are casting lots for your robes."

July 20, 1914, Slepnyovo
Translation by Judith Hemschemeyer

Война объявлена

Владимир Маяковский

«Вечернюю! Вечернюю! Вечернюю!
Италия! Германия! Австрия!»
И на площадь, мрачно очерченную чернью,
багровой крови пролилась струя!

Морду в кровь разбила кофейня,
зверьим криком багрима:
«Отравим кровью игры Рейна!
Громами ядер на мрамор Рима!»

С неба изодранного о штыков жала,
10 слёзы звезд просеивались, как мука в сите,
и подошвами сжатая жалость визжала:
«Ах, пустите, пустите, пустите!»

Бронзовые генералы на граненом цоколе
молили: «Раскуйте, и мы поедем!»
Прощающейся конницы поцелуи цокали,
и пехоте хотелось к убийце — победе.

Громоздящемуся городу уродился во сне
хохочущий голос пушечного баса,
а с запада падает красный снег
20 сочными клочьями человечьего мяса.

Вздувается у площади за ротой рота,
у злящейся на лбу вздуваются вены.
«Постойте, шашки о шелк кокоток
вытрем, вытрем в бульварах Вены!»

Газетчики надрывались: «Купите вечернюю!
Италия! Германия! Австрия!»
А из ночи, мрачно очерченной чернью,
багровой крови лилась и лилась струя.

20 июля 1914 г.

War's Declared
Vladimir Mayakovsky

"Evening papers! Evening papers! Evening papers!
Italy! Germany! Austria!" they scream.
And on the square, in its gloomy black drapery
crimson blood poured and poured in a stream.

The coffee-house smashed up its face, noisy,
blood-shot with bestial yells:
"With blood the frolics of the Rhine let's poison!
Blast the marble of Rome with shells!"

From the heavens shredded by bayonet stings,
like flour from a sieve, the star-tears strained,
and pity, squashed under boot-heels, poor thing,
screamed "Let me go!" again and again.

Bronze generals from their pedestals roared:
"Unshackle us, and we'll ride in a drove!"
Cavalry's farewell kisses were heard,
towards killer victory infantry strove.

To the lumbering city in a monstrous nightmare
the guffawing bass of cannon seemed to crash.
In the West, crimson snow fell earthward, frightening
in juicy slivers of human flesh.

Company after company swells on the square,
veins swell up on its forehead in anger:
"Wait, we'll wipe our sabers yet there
on courtesans' silk in the boulevards of Vienna!"

Newsboys went hoarse: "Buy the evening papers!"
"Italy! Germany! Austria!" they screamed.
And out of the night in its gloomy black drapery
crimson blood poured and poured in a stream.

20 July 1914
Translation by Dorian Rottenberg

Я сам
Владимир Владимирович Маяковский

Война

Принял взволнованно. Сначала только с декоративной, с шумовой стороны. Плакаты заказные и, конечно, вполне военные. Затем стих. «Война объявлена».

Август

Первое сражение. Вплотную встал военный ужас. Война отвратительна. Тыл ещё отвратительней. Чтобы сказать о войне – надо её видеть. Пошёл записываться добровольцем. Не позволили. Нет благонадёжности.

И у полковника Модля оказалась одна хорошая идея.

Зима

Отвращение и ненависть к войне. «Ах, закройте, закройте глаза газет» и другие.

Интерес к искусству пропал вовсе.

I Myself
Vladimir Mayakovsky

War

Took it with agitation. First only in the decorative, noisy aspect. Posters made to order and, of course, about the war. Then a poem. "War's Declared."

August

First battle. The horror of war stared me in the face. War is disgusting. The rear is even more disgusting. To speak about the war – one must see it. Went to enroll as a volunteer. Didn't accept me. Unreliable.

Even Colonel Model[1] had one good idea.

Winter

Disgust and hatred for war. "Ach, shut their eyes, shut the newspapers' eyes!" and others.

Lost all interest in art.

First published in Russian: 1922
Translation by Boris Dralyuk

1. Chief of the Moscow secret police.

ИЗД. НОВ. КРИВ. ЗЕРКАЛО.

Postcard from 1914
UNC Prerevolutionary Postcard Collection

Before she fled to the West in 1919, Teffi was a genuine literary star in Russia, a favorite of both Nicholas II and Lenin. Unfortunately, her writing was neglected for many decades; she was often dismissed as simply a satirist. "Yavdokha" proves how far-ranging her literary gifts really were.

Yavdokha
Nadezhda Teffi

For A D Nyurenberg

On Sunday, on his way from the village, Trifon the miller's hand turned in at the hollow for Yavdokha's little hut, where he gave the old woman a letter.

"'S from your son in th'army."

There she stood, this old woman – long and skinny, spine hunched, eyes open wide and blinking – but she wouldn't take the letter.

"Maybe hit ain't for me?"

"The letterman said hit's for Yavdokha the woodswoman. Take it. 'S from your son in th'army."

At that the old woman took the letter and turned it over and over, feeling it with her rough fingers, the nails all chipped.

"You read what it says – maybe hit ain't for me."

Trifon handled the letter a bit, too; then gave it back to her.

"But I can't read. Them there in the village will read it for you."

With that he left.

Yavdokha stood by her little hut a bit longer, blinking.

The hut was a little one that had taken root. The ground reached right up to the little window with its shards of iridescent glass. But unlike the hut, the old woman was long. That, evidently, is why fate had bent her spine – after all, it couldn't just leave her outdoors.

Yavdokha blinked a little more, went back into the hut and tucked the letter behind the blackened icon.

Then she went out to the boar.

The boar lived in a leaky shed attached to the hut, so that at night-time Yavdokha could hear whenever the boar was scratching its flank against the wall.

And she would think, lovingly:

"Scratch away! Scratch away! You'll be gobbled up come the Lord's nativity, then you won't scratch yourself no more."

And it was for the boar's sake that she'd get herself up in the morning, put a thick canvas mitt on her left hand, take an old sickle worn to a thread and go cut the strong, stringy nettles growing along the wayside.

During the day she would graze the boar in the hollow; in the evening she would drive it back to the shed, scolding loudly, like a real matron with a real, well-run household where – praise the Lord! – everything was as it should be.

It was a long time since she had seen her son. He was working in the city, far away. But now he had sent this letter from "th'army." It meant that they'd got him. It meant he was at the war. It meant he wouldn't be sending any money for the holiday. It meant there would be no bread.

Yavdokha went over to the boar, blinked a few times and said:

"I have a son, Panas. He sended me a letter from th'army."

After this she began to feel easier. But that night she couldn't sleep, and towards morning the road began to reverberate with the sound of heavy footsteps.

The old woman got up and looked through the peephole. There were soldiers going past – a great many of them, grey, quiet, unspeaking. "Where they going? What for? And why so quiet? Why don't they say something?"

She grew afraid. Lying down, she pulled the covers over her head, and as soon as the sun came up she got ready to go to the village.

She went outside, this long, skinny old woman, looked round her and blinked a few times. This is where the soldiers had passed the night before. The road was all sticky and mucky, as if it had been pounded with a mortar, and the grass along the roadside had been beaten to the ground.

"They flattened the boar's nettles. Right flattened them!"

And off she went, kneading the mud with her skinny legs and wooden staff for a distance of eight *versts*.[1]

In the village a celebration was underway: the girls were weaving a bridal wreath for Lazy Eye Ganka, who was to be married to Nikanor, son of Khromenko. This Nikanor was going to the war, but the elderly Khromenkos needed a hand round the house. If Nikanor got killed, it would be too late – which is why the girls were weaving a wreath for Lazy Eye Ganka.

In Ganka's hut it was stuffy. It smelled of sour bread and sour sheepskin.

The girls were crowded onto a bench round the table – red, sweaty and browless. They were fussing over scrap flowers and ribbons, picking and choosing among them. And with all the might of their healthy workers' bodies, they were madly wailing out a call-and-answer song.

Faces fierce, nostrils flaring, they sang like they were hard at work. But this was a song of the fields and the wide open spaces that could be heard straight from one field to the next. Here, in the crowded hut, the song was squashed and deformed. It buzzed and thrashed around the tiny clay-sealed windows, unable to get out. And the women and young men clustered round just squinted, as though the wind was in their eyes.

"Hoy! Hey! Ho-o-o! Hoy! Hey! Ho-o-o!"

The bass was roaring, and whatever the words, they all sounded like "Hoy-hey-ho-o-o!" Oh, what a noise!

Yavdokha pressed in through the door. A woman turned to face her.

"I have a son. Panas," said Yavdokha. "He sended a letter from th'army."

---

1. A *verst* is just over a kilometer, so 8 *versts* is just under five miles.

The woman didn't reply, but maybe she just didn't hear, the girls were making such a noise.

Yavdokha decided to wait and found herself a little spot in the corner.

Then the girls fell silent – abruptly, as if they'd been gagged – and over by the door a violin began to scrape like a cock with the croup, and galloping behind it, as though in a hurry to overtake it, came a tambourine. The crowd pressed back towards the door, and into the middle of the hut stepped two flat-chested girls with exaggerated bellies in straight waistless corsets. They hugged each other, then began to dance, stamping and bobbing as if they were tripping. Twice they circled round.

Then a young man emerged from the crowd. Flinging back his oily locks of fair hair, he squatted and started going round, extending and retracting his crooked legs in their bast shoes. He didn't look like he was dancing so much as crawling, clumsily and pitifully, like a crippled freak who would gladly stand if only he could.

He went round the circle, then straightened up and squeezed back into the crowd.

Suddenly everyone began calling:

"Come out, Granny Sakhfeya! Come out, Granny Sakhfeya!"

A little old woman with a warm scarf wrapped round her head waved her arm angrily and shook her head – no way was she going to come out.

Those who didn't know any better asked in surprise, "Why go picking on an old granny?"

But those who were in the know shouted out:

"Come out, Granny Sakhfeya!"

And then the old woman's face creased and she began to laugh. She turned towards the icon.

"Well, all right then. Let me just ask the Lord's forgiveness first." Crossing herself, she kneeled down before the icon and said three times:

"Forgive me, oh Lord, forgive me, oh Lord, forgive me, oh Lord!"

Then she turned back and said with a smirk:

"Well, I've reckoned for my sin."

And was there ever something to reckon for! The way she held her hands on her hips, the way she winked, the way she cocked her head... Whoopee!

A gangling young man leapt out and began to pretzel his bast-shod legs. But no one was looking at him. They were all looking at Sakhfeya. At that moment she wasn't even dancing, merely standing and waiting her turn, waiting for the young man to bound over to her. The young man was the only one dancing and she was just waiting, but all the dance was in her, not him. He may have been pretzeling his bast-shod legs, but her every vein was humming, every bone playing, every drop of blood surging. Don't look at him – look at her! And then it was her turn. She swung round, leaped up – and she was off! Whoopee!

This old woman knew what she was doing when she begged the Lord's forgiveness. Yes sir, a sin like that would cost you dearly in the next world.

But Yavdokha was squashed into her little corner and couldn't see a thing – which was just as well, because goings on like these *nobody* ought to see!

Once she'd caught her breath, she made her way to the outer room.

Here she found the bridegroom Nikanor tormenting a dog with a stick.

"Nikanor! Maybe you can read. My son Panas in th'army sended me a letter."

The bridegroom hesitated a moment – he didn't want to be distracted from his entertainment. He hesitated, then threw the stick aside and took the old woman's letter. He tore a corner off the top, peeked inside, then carefully slipped a finger in and ripped the envelope open.

"Yes, it really is a letter. Now listen up: 'Auntie Yavdokha, my respects and the Lord's health to you. We keep marching on and on and we're very tired but not terrible tired. Your son Apanasy's gone to the next world. Maybe he got hurt but don't you hope 'cause he's gone to the next world. From Filipp Melnikov, who you know.' That's all."

"Pilipp?" asked the old woman, making sure she heard right.

"Pilipp."

Then she thought a little and asked:

"Who was it got hurt? Pilipp?"

"Who knows? Maybe it was Pilipp. You can't hardly tell. A lot of people's getting roughed up. Hit's the war."

"Hit's the war," agreed the old woman. "But maybe you could read some more?"

"I don't have time now. Come back Sunday and I'll read some more."

"Well all right then, I'll come back on Sunday."

She tucked the letter in her bosom and poked her nose into the hut.

"Well, what is it?" asked a young man and pushed her away with his elbow, the same young man who had danced so freakishly earlier on. "What do you want?"

"Hit's from my son, from Panas – a letter from th'army. Pilipp Melnikov got hurt or maybe not. A lot of people's getting roughed up. Hit's the war."

And that evening, as she was approaching her little hut, sliding along the splattered, slimy road, she was thinking two thoughts – one sad, the other untroubled.

The sad thought was:

"They flattened the boar's nettles."

And the untroubled one:

"Panas sended a letter. That means he'll send some money, too. When he sends the money, I'll buy some bread."

And that was all.

First published in Russian: 1916
Translated by Anne Marie Jackson

Мой ответ
Игорь Северянин

Ещё не значит быть сатириком –
Давать озлобленный совет
Прославленным поэтам-лирикам
Искать и воинских побед...

Неразлучаемые с Музою
Ни под водою, ни в огне,
Боюсь, мы будем лишь обузою
Своим же братьям на войне.

Мы избалованы вниманием,
И наши ли, pardon, грехи,
Когда идут шестым изданием
Иных «ненужные» стихи?!

– Друзья! Но если в день убийственный
Падёт последний исполин,
Тогда ваш нежный, ваш единственный,
Я поведу вас на Берлин!

1914 Зима

My Reply
Igor Severyanin

It does not mean that one's a satirist,
if one advises – piqued and cruel –
that an illustrious poet-lyricist
should seek out martial glory too...

We and the Muse cannot be parted,
be it in water or by fire,
and fear we'll only be a burden
to our own brethren in the war.

We have been spoiled by much attention –
pardonnez-nous, is it our sin,
when they release a sixth edition
of "needless" poems by another hand?

– But friends! If on a murderous day
our last great giant's slain,
then I myself – your gentle one, your nonpareil,
will lead you to Berlin!

1914 Winter
Translation by Boris Dralyuk

Воздушный витязь

Сергей Городецкий

Памяти П. Н. Нестерова

Он взлетел, как в родную стихию,
В голубую воздушную высь,
Защищать нашу матерь Россию, –
Там враги в поднебесье неслись.

Он один был, воитель крылатый,
А врагов было три корабля,
Но отвагой и гневом объятый,
Он догнал их. Притихла земля.

И над первым врагом, быстр и светел,
Он вознесся, паря, как орел.
Как орел, свою жертву наметил
И стремительно в битву пошел.

В этот миг он, наверное, ведал
Над бессильным врагом торжество,
И крылатая дева Победа
Любовалась полетом его.

Воевала земля, но впервые
Небеса охватила война.
Как удары грозы огневые,
Был бесстрашен удар летуна.

И низринулся враг побежденный!..
Но нашел в том же лютом бою,
Победитель, судьбой пораженный,
Молодую, могилу свою.

Победителю вечная слава!
Слава витязям синих высот!
Ими русская крепнет держава,
Ими русская сила растет.

Их орлиной бессмертной отвагой
Пробивается воинству след,
Добывается русское благо,
Начинается песня побед.

Слава войску крылатому, слава!
Слава всем удальцам-летунам!
Слава битве средь туч величавой!
Слава русским воздушным бойцам!

1914

Knight of the Air
Sergey Gorodetsky

to the memory of P. N. Nesterov

He soared, as if into his native element,
into the blue and airy heights,
in order to defend our Mother Russia –
enemies had swarmed into our skies.

He was alone, a wingèd warrior,
facing three enemy ships,
but, embraced by courage and anger,
he chased them down. Our land had peace.

Quick and bright, he flew like an eagle,
rising above his prey.
Like an eagle, he spotted the first enemy,
and promptly charged into the fray.

At that moment he likely knew triumph
over an enemy robbed of its might,
and Victory, the wingèd maiden,
admired his marvelous flight.

Our land saw fighting, but first
the war had seized our skies.
Like fiery thunder bursts
were the flyer's fearless strikes.

The vanquished enemy plunged!..
But in that battle fierce and brave,
the victor, wounded by fate,
found his early grave.

Eternal glory to the victor!
To the knights of the blue heights!
They add to Russia's power –
they strengthen the Russian state.

Their deathless, eagle-like courage
breaks paths for our warring men,
secures good fortune for Russia,
commences the victory song.

Glory to the wingèd army!
Glory to our daring flyers!
Glory to that majestic battle in the clouds!
Glory to Russia's aerial fighters!

1914
Translation by Boris Dralyuk

"Primitive Russian Gas Mask"
Capt. Donald C. Thompson (1917)

Ilya Ehrenburg was surely one of the most versatile of Soviet writers. He was, among other things, one of the most important frontline correspondents and Soviet propagandists of the Second World War, and it is interesting to compare the patriotism and anti-German character of his writings from that period with the tone of his reporting on the First World War.

The Face of War
Ilya Ehrenburg

Introduction to the First Edition

For five years it has been a part of our lives. It travels through cities and lands, sometimes fearsome and violent, dispensing death, and sometimes weary, distant, a mere evocation of the horrific battles that fill our hearts with bitter memories and foreboding. There's a great irony in our lives: we have grown accustomed to it; we have gotten used to the unbearable. The road to our Golgotha is so long that we've come to measure it with mile markers. It is an ancient and mythical time we seem to invoke when we say, "That was before the war." We have made a new normalcy and found a new comfort in the crucible. The war is with us and inside us, but we do not know where. Its mysterious face is obscured under a thick cloak. We have gotten so good at living with it, so used to its faceless skeleton, that we do not even notice its mystery.

My fragmentary and cryptic notes are sketches of the war's features that revealed themselves by accident, in fleeting moments. There has been a lot written about war, perhaps even too much, and the majority of this writing is an attempt to pass judgment on the war. The writers were *a priori* "for" or "against" it. Some have tried to justify the war (Charles Le Goffic, Paul Claudel, V. Ropshin,[1] Barzini, Richard Dehmel), others were righteously enraged (Barbusse, Raulland, Mayakovsky), but only a few spoke of its countless visages in a living and tremulous voice (Fyodor Stepun, Sofia Fedorchenko, Paul Lintier). Perhaps my notes will serve to add to their books.

I have no wish to prove or disprove anything. If I thought I knew what war was, I would be able to elevate or expose it. But I only know hundreds of its different faces, and am ignorant of her true face.

As every day at war, another war was being fought in parallel, its theater was the soul of every human being, and its antagonists – the primordial enemies, the good and evil. The total chaos of human emotion and thought stood out with a special power and clarity. People climbed to the previously unknown pinnacles of spirit, and tumbled into its abysses. At war, one could learn to love mankind, and also to hate it with a new hatred. The outer dressings of the soul fell away, one's amazed eyes beheld the pure nudity of the human heart, and it turned out to be more mysterious and complex than any of its previous incarnations.

My book is about France and often about the French people. Much there is owed to a national character that is foreign to us, but never has there been a time when two nations were closer to each other – bound by a single hatred and a single love – than we were in the war years when we set out to destroy each other. A reader who has seen the war at the Russian front will, perhaps, find days of his own life in this book.

Distant offshoots of a single plant will come together at the root and in the last bloom. It would be a mistake to hold the French accountable for any of the monstrous visions of war I described. I happened to see Frenchmen; others witnessed Germans or Russians. But the war is the sin of all humanity and mankind's absolution. It was not my intent to write a history of war or to identify the guilty. The accounts of German brutality on the occupied territories, or the French treatment of the "colored" or Russian

1. V. Ropshin – pen-name of Boris Savenkov, Russian writer and revolutionary terrorist (1878-1925).

units, or Russians' own violence in sacked France are not political maneu-
vers or legal analysis. These are merely visions of different human tribes
drunk on the same wine of madness.

The war seemed to everyone sudden and impossible. Its horrors met
with bewilderment, and many spoke with outrage of the debasement of
civilized man. But was pre-war Europe not ruled by the same principles of
clear-eyed cruelty, mechanical madness, soulless will? The crowds of Parisian boulevards come to mind: people moving like wind-up toys, hypocrit-
ical abbots and orators calling audiences to battle for a piece of pie. I recall
an execution at Le Santé Prison, the carefree girls, street-stands selling
pastries, the boisterous festival around the guillotine, and amoebic poets
who declaimed, that same night, verses about the dolphins of the Trianon
Palace at Versailles. I remember the parliament and the university, the bor-
dellos and the stock-market, the red marches and the balls. This I know:
war did not descend suddenly. Europe had carried it in its womb for years.

Neither has the war ended. The apocalyptic scroll has been unrolled and
the seals have been broken. Terrible forces have been summoned to life,
and they will not be appeased by a handful of diplomats at a conference.
The great whirlwind has sucked up mankind into its maw, and it will abide
no human will. What are our generals, politicians, sages and tribunes in
the face of this wind of destruction? The war goes on. It changes shapes; it
comes from the front to the cities, to the villages, it enters into our homes.
Whether it's nation against nation or class against class – the same thing
is happening under a different set of banners. War has atomized itself, it
dissolved, and if it did indeed die as a pursuit of governments, it is alive and
well in our individual hearts. Who will snatch the flaming sword from the
pale rider's hand? I don't know. This I know: evil will not be defeated with
another evil; war will not annihilate war. Destruction knows no end; it is a
fiery circle, and we are its prisoners.

Kyiv, March 4, 1919

The Outward Face

I

Commonly, if one were to ask, "What can one see at war?" the answer would be, "One doesn't see anything." I think it is not quite so. Rather, at war, one sees "nothing" – the non-being, the void. There's the brown, naked earth; straight lines of dead barbed wire; thin threads of trenches, stretched according to plan. Not a tree, not a seed flying in the wind – everything has been rooted out, splintered, turned to dust. Somewhere, there are people burrowed in underground holes, but one can't see them; no thing that lives, moves or breathes dares show itself, dares tread upon this doomed earth. More powerfully than the ocean or the desert, war speaks of the power of the void. The eye drowns, and the heart begins to comprehend something on the far side of being. Man, still living and breathing, begins to live his dying hour.

II

How beautiful and appealing war was in the paintings of the old French and Dutch masters! Rearing horses, pennants fluttering in the wind, billowing clouds of smoke! There's the drummer drumming the call, and the general's face is proud, and his hand flies up with such magnificence, and the soldiers in emerald or ruby coats run to victory. This is war as a child's game or an old-fashioned opera. Often, walking through the rain-sodden trenches and looking at the gray soldiers, the cannons and the machine guns, I wondered, will there ever be an artist who can render this?

Now I am looking at a collection of war drawings by the French artist Joseph Fernand Henri Léger. Before, I felt indifferent as I passed through exhibits of contemporary military painters; I was indifferent as I studied great photographs or read excellent poems about war. I knew: this was it, but I couldn't recognize it. Now, I am trembling as I leaf through Leger's strange, mysterious works. Yes, I have not seen anything like this, but also – this is all I have seen. Leger is a cubist; his work is sometimes schematic, sometimes unsettling in its endless fragmentation of the entire visible universe, but it is here – the face of the war, crucified, spliced with the artist's cruel knife, and yet somehow reconstituted at the edge of perception and therefore visible. Leger's drawings do not portray anything personal or individual, because at war, there is no Jean or Karl, there are no Germans or Frenchmen, but only the mass of ourselves, humanity and the man.

Or perhaps there isn't even that, since all the images speak of a single master: the machine. Soldiers in their helmets, horses' croups, stove-pipes of field-kitchens, the wheels of the cannons – these are all parts of a single great mechanism. There are no colors: everything loses its color at work, the cannons as much as the soldiers' faces – everything turns ashen. The lines are straight; the planes intersect at clean angles; the drawings look like blueprints – everything freewheeling, whimsical, endearingly irregular has been obliterated. There's no room for daydreams, sleep, desire at war. War is a well-equipped factory for the obliteration of mankind. We are but tiny gears that spin and then stop, unable to fit the entire magnificent edifice into our limited field of vision.

The drawings are snippets of the factory's plans, copied surreptitiously by a kind Frenchman, and the builder and master of this factory is known to the faithful as the Prince of Darkness.

III

They say a handful of all-powerful men rule us: Kaiser Wilhelm, Lloyd George, Marshal Joffre, the diplomats, the owners of the arms factories, the generals, the stock brokers. If only! For these are all men – each one of them has a living organ beating under his vest, each was a boy once, each knows longing, and each will die. But no, it's not men that rule the war. Today, I have seen our true masters.

At dusk, I was traveling along the road near Arras. The flat, meager lands of Artois spread out on both sides of the road, crisscrossed with white country lanes. Along these lanes moved, in an endless chain, heavy trucks. Some of them were transporting soldiers "there," others were bringing the wounded "from there," and some carried guns, shells, meat carcasses, bread. They stopped at intersections to wait for a signal from a soldier directing traffic: a flick of a flag from the tiny master of ceremonies. Each truck had an emblem – a dragon, a snake, a bird – and each had a name and number. Each soldier also had a name, and each wore a bracelet with a number so his corpse could be identified. But the soldiers were mere foot-servants of the mighty trucks; their job was to fuss around the big guns, and pull the cord, to feed the machine guns, and to pull the triggers. They would serve the machine and feed their flesh to it. I watched for an hour, then two, and the trucks never stopped coming, and hundreds of people worked constantly fixing and patching the roads that couldn't bear the nation's march. The trucks looked black against the pink sunset. I wanted to fall to my knees, to show obeisance to the forces that compel Wilhelm as much as they do a poor Senegalese recruit.

IV

The first time I saw a tank, I was taken aback: it was both magnificent and utterly repulsive. Perhaps it looked like an enormous insect that roamed the earth in primordial times. The tank was painted in many colors for camouflage, and its flanks turned into abstract paintings. It crawled very slowly, like a caterpillar, climbing over trenches and holes, chewing through barbed wire and bushes. Its feelers – three-inch cannons and machine guns – moved a little. The thing was a bizarre combination of the archaic and the ultra-American, Noah's ark and a twenty-first-century bus. Inside the tank were people – twelve pathetic pygmies, who were convinced, in their naiveté, that they drove the machine.

I saw nine tanks close in on the German trenches before an attack. The Germans unleashed a barrage of fire, but the machines advanced as if they didn't notice, inevitable and incomprehensible. It was a prophet's warning come to life: men have summoned evil spirits, and can banish them no more.

V

Hundreds of painters are employed in camouflaging cannons and trucks, manufacturing colorful rugs that are thrown over entire artillery positions, or arranging tree branches and painted canvas to mask roads. Here's a fake tree, hollow inside, and a fake dead horse: at night, these will be brought to the front lines to replace an actual birch-tree and an actual dead horse, and will house scouts. At first, the camouflage people painted everything brown, but they soon discovered that the shapes of trucks and other objects stood out. Now, the painters break up a single plane into large blocks of color which, from afar, obscure the shape of the object. Every day they come up with new tricks, adjusting to the yellow tint of Picard clay, Champagne's chalky soil, or the green of the Argonne woods. To become unseen, to blend with the earth – or, rather, to have the earth swallow you – that is the goal of this macabre masquerade, in which every mistake costs a life. People become like worms that live in the dirt and strive to remain looking like dirt any time they peek out.

Not far from the camouflage workshops, in a different building, people with magnifying glasses labor to decipher sinister images that look like Picasso's tangled drawings. These are aerial photographs. Sharp-eyed birds crisscross the skies above the recalcitrant human worms, exposing their burrows. Here a trained eye finds a thin line of a trench, here it spots a black dot – an artillery position, perhaps? Men compare hundreds of pictures, tracking down each suspicious blot. And the other men dig deeper, become even more unseen, more gray, drop their flags and lose their drums, and the queen of the masquerade walks across the field with her buttons sheathed in gray fabric – Lady War.

VI

Work never stops in the foggy Calais; the labor is relentless, dogged. The heart of war beats day and night. Here's a bakery turning out two hundred thousand loaves every day for the army. Here's a cobbler's, where old boots, torn at the front, are recut and remade. Next to it is a hand-grenade factory. The warehouses are truly gigantic: hundreds of steamships deliver frozen mutton from Australia, flour from Canada, tea from Ceylon, New Zealand cheese, and men – all for the War's next meal. The supply stores carry everything from heavy artillery to pocket mirrors, from the gadgets that measure the speed of poison gas to stationery printed with forget-me-nots. Twenty-three hundred different parts for different makes of automobiles are issued according to individual ID numbers. The order slips read, "#617 for large-caliber tank for Army X" or "steering wheel #1301 for motorcycle for the headquarters of Y division." Thousands of workers service the workshops and stores. Cross the English Channel, or go to Lyon, Cherbourg, Saint-Étienne to the plants that manufacture shells, trucks, and airplanes and everywhere you will find the raging fire of smelting furnaces, the roar and screech of machines, the sweaty, soot-blackened faces of men. Battles are just the results of all this work; victories are a tally of shells made and mutton-chops delivered. Banners, medals, tales of heroism – those are all voices of the past, War reminiscing about its youth. It has traded David's slingshot for the long inventory of Calais warehouses.

VII

We have been walking for a long time. Three hours, I think. We have covered more than ten kilometers, but the terrifying vision does not loosen its grip. It is not a mirage, a fancy or a dream – this is the truth. There had been meadows, fields, villages, people and animals, life. Now there is nothing. Now there is death. The Apocalypse refers to this place as the Armageddon; we call it the Battle of the Ancre. The maps tell us: here was one village, and over there another, but there's not a stone left of those places. The stones have been ground into dust. Today, on a May morning, one cannot find a single tuft of grass or a wisp of a leaf. The earth lies tortured, deformed – dead. Even the shape of the hills is changed, and the fast-flowing Ancre lost its original bed, spilling into gigantic hollows and ravines. The brown clay is pocked with sink-holes, filled with murky rainwater that makes them look like pus-wounds. Terrible things sprout in these fields: among rusty bits of wire, broken rifles and shards of artillery shells, the earth disgorges remains of the combatants – rusty, bloated boots, skulls still wearing their helmets... How many of them are here? I cannot tell, they are without number. At sea, when one feels sick, one looks for a stable point to look at, a bit of solid ground. Here, I start looking at the sky, with its fleeting clouds – it is the only thing that is still solid, something to hold on to.

Two skulls stick out of the dirt in front of us: one is wearing a flatter helmet – he was British – while the other one was German. Enemies not so long ago, they now appear to be grinning with the same horrible grin, no longer men's faces, but skulls. We stop, look at each other, seeming to grin ourselves. Suddenly, a living thing catapults at us from the mud: a common cat. She leaps at us with a screech, but dashes away when threatened with a stick. (It's common to run into cats that have gone wild at the front: they feed on corpses.) The skulls grin.

My companion is an English officer with a child's blue eyes, a long-legged and quiet man. He hasn't said anything the entire way; I was beginning to think he never speaks. But now, either because of the skulls or because of the cat, he suddenly begins to sing, not quite in tune and with a funny accent. It's an old song:

Quand les lilas refleuriront
Dans ces vallées nous reviendrons...[2]

He sings and steps over corpses. Lord only knows if he's laughing at me, at himself, at all of us, or if the gray disheveled cat truly reminded him that even in this valley of death, the fragrant lilacs will bloom again one day.

VIII

At the bank of the Somme, I see two skeletons – a man and a horse. The battle happened three months ago, and the wind and the rains have since stripped the bodies down to the white, clean bones. The man still has his

2. "When the lilacs bloom again, we'll walk again these valleys" — a popular song at the time.

46 helmet, his leather belt and his boots. The horse is saddled and bridled. It is all that remains.

IX

The eye can forget the sight of war, the corpses and the skeletons, the chunks of flesh, the annihilation, the graveyards. The ear can forget the war's sounds, the rumble of heavy artillery, the meow and shrill of the shrapnel, the tutting of the machine guns, the roar of the soldiers running into the enemy's bayonets, the groans of the wounded left in front of the lines. But even if the visions fade, and the terrible voices grow silent, one remembers – until one's dying hour – the inextirpable smell of war. Scorched earth, human feces, and the corpses that crawl out of the dirt on a muggy July day produce a coy, sickening smell. It cannot be forgotten.

X

An enormous military cemetery in Châlons-sur-Marne. At the gate, four cannons are still menacing someone. Long rows of identical crosses – how many are there? Someone has counted: about fifteen hundred.

It's crowded, each soldier given no more space than in closed ranks. No flowers or wreaths, only the government-issue tricolor circle on every cross. Someone lined up the dead into battalions, as if there were no peace beyond the grave for them, as if they still had to march into another battle.

Somewhere else there are graves that can soothe pain with their quiet dignity. Somewhere else there is grass, and sun, and women's tears and birds. But this bare field, this parade of the murdered does not speak of eternal peace. It reminds us again of our baseness, of our insignificance. We pass through life ID'd and numbered, tiny screws, cogs and wheels in an incomprehensible machine; miniscule pawns moved for an inscrutable purpose and then taken out altogether by the unknowable Player's hand.

I

August 2nd, the day war was declared. Moving from Holland to Paris, I had to cross the French border on foot.

It was dawning as we walked through the fields, between walls of golden, heavy wheat. Larks sang. My companions, French men who'd been mobilized, walked in silence. A herd of cows crossed the empty road, and a bell rang dolefully. In the distance, we saw a French border guard. For some reason, he fired a shot into the air, and the sudden, dry sound of it was frightening and new in the peaceful quiet of a country morning. Soldiers began singing *La Marseillaise*. Talk started of first battles, of the thousands already dead, fantastic talk, boastful and scared at the same time. We met refugees walking in the opposite direction – Germans, fleeing France, with bundles and children.

"*Eh bien! C'est la guerre!*" the border guard said thoughtfully.[3]

I turned around for one last look at the white road, the wheat bending under its own weight, and the distant chimney-smoke of the village. I didn't know then that just a few days later, artillery would torch these farms and cavalry would tromp across these fields. I had no way of knowing that war was not something that lasted a month or a year, that the clear morning separated two entire epochs, and the days of the past, carefree and easy, would be no more. I had no way of knowing that I would lose everything I loved in this war, and more than that: my ability to experience joy and to believe. I did not know any of this, and still I looked back with a vague apprehension, with inexplicable turmoil, as if I were bidding farewell to life itself.

----

3. Well, this is war!

II

A storm indeed!

It is very hot in our cattle car. There are about thirty *Zouaves* here.[4] They drink red wine.

Every fifteen minutes a military train passes in the opposite direction. Soldiers lean out of their cars and shout something we can't quite hear. The stations are crowded with those departing and those seeing them off. People hand more wine to our *Zouaves*. Our train crawls; the engine moans mournfully. On the platforms, the embankments and at the crossings, tearful women wave their handkerchiefs at the trains. Someone chalked "Pleasure Train to Berlin" on the side of our car, but no one thinks it's very funny. The men drink and sing "Mariette, Mariette." Abuzz with wine, the heat, and all the shouting, they don't really know anything, don't think, don't remember. War? Berlin? Death? Damn it, let's have another! Anything not to think! The song goes on, and the trains pass, and the women weep, and the wheels groan – *quo vadis? Quo vadis?* And the evil, merciless sun blasts everyone with heavy heat.

Paris is in chaos. The entire city seems to have come to the railway stations, crowded under the glass domes. There are paper flags, and brave songs, and forced jokes, and tears, tears, tears. Shops are closed. Cafes are locked at eight. Who has it in him to sell, to work, to party? The storm is spinning, sucking everyone in. An old lady sobs:

"They took them both! Both!"

A battalion suddenly comes from around the corner. Where are they going? East, of course! The bayonets are clean, no blood yet – only colorful flowers tacked on.

"*Allons, enfants de la Patrie!*"[5] The song carries them forward, compels them. It's such a strange song; only the French know how to sing it in such

---

4. *Zouave* was the title given to certain light infantry regiments in the French Army, normally serving in French North Africa.

5. "Arise, children of the fatherland!" A line from the *Marseillaise*.

a way that death itself retreats in awe. When we sing it, it comes out sad and funereal.

A small street resonates with a hundred foot-falls.

Someone groans in a doorway: "Louis, my Louis!"

Newspaper boys shout, "Victory!"

Life has ended, and all of this was before – far behind us. I ask a friend of mine, a painter who is about to depart for Belfort, "Where are you storing your works?"

He looks at me with distant, unseeing eyes.

"My works? What difference does it make?"

That is also in the past, and the past now appears useless and laughable. Perhaps we didn't really live, before? Or are we not living now? I can't tell. Our homes and affairs, paintings and books, our great legacy – all of this is suddenly vanished, gone. A magician waved his wand and turned gold into dust. We have lost everything, and the wind is blowing, blowing the dust hard, and carries us with it.

"Kill as many Krauts as you can!" shouts a blonde girl with a child's smile. "Kill them! Kill them!"

On the corner, a very young officer is saying goodbye to a woman in black. She holds him in a long, hopeless embrace. I catch his words, exalted and tender:

"It is such a joy! I sacrifice it all!"

Night falls.

III

Those who were left behind led a peculiar existence in those first weeks. Everyone felt as if they were either constantly waiting at the station for a certain train to pull in, or were holding a vigil at a sickbed: will the patient get better, or die? People fell on newspapers with prayerful thirst and drank the poison of hatred and madness. People endured the hours between the morning and the evening telegrams. We abandoned our usual affairs, we wrote letters, put flag-pins into maps and waited. When the first wounded appeared, passersby in the street would stop, their arguments and jokes frozen on their lips. At night we dozed off fitfully, our souls tuned in to the ominous thundering from "over there." The days were hot and humid. The sun rose and set as always, the weeks ticked by. But people were anguished with the anguish of death.

How did this happen? How did catastrophe become routine, death – unremarkable, murder – commonplace, war – an everyday pastime? In the fall, trees take days to shed their leaves, and in the spring it takes weeks for the snows to melt, and suddenly we notice thawed, warm dirt or a denuded orchard. We got used to the war day after day, and then one day we looked up – and were surprised.

War? Yes, of course, it's there, but one is expected at the office, and one's about to finish a very interesting report indeed. Gaston Calmette[6] has been shot? How terrible! And we're going to see the new *revue* at the Bouffe to-night... People returned to their usual business, their old entertainments, although everything was slightly poisoned by the invisible whiffs of death from the Marne or the Ain, and something died forever in people's hearts on August 2nd. But the new, wartime way of life took root very quickly, with its regimented days, its own preoccupations and levities. Life held its own, and the great lightning bolts that scorched the hair of some and blinded others, did not strike into its ancient heart.

IV

Some left, others stayed behind. Some saw the war, and others read about it in the papers. They will never understand each other. A husband looks away from his wife for an instant, in the midst of the deepest intimacy, and suddenly remembers something he knows *she* will never know and will never understand – and she's a stranger to him.

Of course, soldiers who came on leave were often upset with the very appearance of the rear. I have seen them stare hatefully at the cafés where

6. Gaston Calmette, prominent journalist and editor of *Le Figaro*, was shot by the second wife of Minister of Finance Joseph Caillaux, whom he reviled in the paper.

people drank their aperitifs through straws at five o'clock, as always; glare at the theaters and gardens, at the perambulating crowds, at everything that, by comparison with the trenches, looks either like heaven or the devil's most vile and twisted lie. But it is the family and friends that stun them most – they are so incomprehensibly alien! What can they talk about? The folks at home have not seen the war; is it us, the soldiers, that have gone blind, or those at home who cannot see? They do not know war, and they can never understand our madness and our wisdom.

A small farm in the South of France. A soldier just came back on leave. The family has dined. He is telling them about the war. His mother, wife, and sisters listen, terrified, exclaiming *oh!* at the scariest parts. Then it's their turn to speak, and what do they say? Well, we can't complain – the grape harvest is good this year. We now sell rabbits to Grasse, at three francs a piece. And did you hear, M-me Sophie's had a baby girl, and Juliette got mixed up with that beanpole Jean...

They have their own affairs, their life – and it had been his life, too, until recently. He wants to tell them of the new thing that he had seen – the thing that overshadows everything. He speaks again. The women sigh again. Soon they begin to yawn. It's been a long day at the farm – time to go to bed. Tomorrow they need to go to market in Grasse, to sell tomatoes. The soldier is restless. He failed to tell them the most important thing, the main thing. His wife puts her arms around him:

"*Mon petit*, let's go to bed..."

He shakes off her embrace and speaks, gruffly, in fragments:

"The war... you don't know what it is... it... it stinks."

V

It was just this morning that I walked across a rusty-brown field, pock-marked with our shelling, and listened to the thunder of our artillery. Just this morning, the only thing I wanted to know was where the attack was being prepared – at the 304th or at Morthomme – and the best way to get to my position and not catch our own fire. Only this morning I was – in mind and in body – *there*. And now I am in Paris; I am sitting on the terrace of a café with the provincial name Closerie de Lilas. Streetlights glimmer on the bluish, rain-washed cobblestones of the square. Noiselessly, like a bat, a car speeds by. A pair of young women walks by, both slim, in trim navy suits. I cannot see their faces, but catch the ineffable drift of perfume. My companion is a French woman painter. She talks about the Blessed John of Ruysbroeck,[7] and something else...

I interrupt, point to the rosy sky, at the bright green of the plantains, the streetlights, the young women: so wonderful!

Suddenly – I don't even recognize it right away – a new emotion wells up in me. I remember everything that is left *back there*, and can no longer rejoice – only regret. Suddenly the people here, and the sky, and Paris, and our conversation become inexpressibly mundane and boring. Life? Of course – but it is only *there*. I stop seeing and hearing; I withdraw. No one can talk to me now. People may walk, argue, read, sleep here, but they cannot be truly living because it is only in the face of death, ducking shells, dissolving in mud, in torment – not *here* – that one can come to know the force, the beauty and wonder of unconquerable life.

VI

It is easy to recognize soldiers who've returned from the front, even when they're dressed in suits and bowler hats. They've been *there* – the evidence of this is a peculiar angularity that peeks from under the mask of a modern cultivated Parisian, the gestures and attitudes of a primitive man, a man who had been returned to his elemental state, and new words – an entire language of war – mixed with sudden silences and inexplicable aloofness.

They return alien, absent-minded. Eventually, they get used to it, re-enter their old routines. On my street, there's Viktor, a ladies' hairdresser. As a dragoon at the front he may have chopped and sliced at his fair share of

7. A Flemish medieval mystic.

Germans, and now he dispenses compliments, so essential to his trade, as he wields the curling iron. A poet I know, Mr. M, used to operate a poison gas diffusion machine; he'd been released and now collects China shepherdesses and writes poems about the gardens of Versailles. Someone is still killing someone somewhere, but they're out of this game. The rules of the game are such that it is best to forget all about it, as quickly as possible; otherwise it is very hard to live. So they forget. Yet, deep in their souls, the visions persist, ineradicable.

Yesterday, I went to visit my friend Mr. L, a painter. He spent two years at the front. We talked a lot about painting, about Diaghilev's ballets and Paul Claudel's new book. There was no war; never had been. Snacks were served. L.'s wife asked for help opening a can. L. shuddered and fell silent. He didn't speak another word for the rest of the evening, just sat there, glum and focused on something elsewhere, clearly deaf to our talk. At the door, he smiled at me:

"There was this time when we came back to the trenches after an attack and I used my bayonet to open a can of food... I didn't see at first that the bayonet was all bloody. But it was ok, we ate anyway. It just all sort of came back..."

I knew what he meant. "All" was much more terrifying than a bloody bayonet. While sitting in his living room, with his charming wife that he adored, with his friends, talking about things dear to his heart, Mr. L suddenly saw the face of war.

VII

My roommate is Serbian. He survived the retreat through Albania, where Austrian airplanes swooped down on columns of unarmed refugees and dropped bombs on them. He was wounded in the head with a bomb fragment. At Saint-Jean de Medua, he and three thousand other Serbs waited for nine days with no food for the steamship to come. Finally, it came, but on its way to Italy the ship was hit and sank. The man spent several hours in the water clinging to a board, and survived. His brother was killed in the war. The Bulgarians hanged his father, and took his mother and both sisters somewhere – he doesn't know where. He is twenty-three years old. He hasn't been killed, hasn't starved, didn't drown and didn't lose his mind. It means he's still alive.

I know how hard he works on being alive. He has been admitted to the Sorbonne, where he studies French literature, is courting a girl and even does athletic gymnastics. He never speaks of the war, and if he does talk about Serbia, he keeps the subjects peaceful and distant: the suckling pig roasted for Christmas or the dear, dirty cafes of his native Kragujevac. I'm sure all his professors and classmates think him a most unremarkable, hardworking young man.

Last night, he knocked on my door.

"Are you asleep yet? May I stay with you for a while? I cannot be alone – it happens quite often now. Usually, I go outside, to the boulevard corner – carriage drivers stay there all night long. I have to tell someone: I hate everything! Mademoiselle U. gave me flowers today, lilies of the valley – I hate them, I stomped on them a minute ago. I read Anatole France today – disgusting! I don't know... I want to know – how do you live? There was a boy at Saint-Jean, he was really hungry, and we had nothing, so he started chewing on his own arm. He shrieked, cried for his Mom... they said he'd gone mad. A friend of mine – he ate dirt. He died. I'm sorry, I'll stop – you've read all this in newspapers already..."

He fell silent and sat there without saying a word for the rest of the night, not really aware of me being there. In the morning, he went to class. He went on living, I go on living, everyone goes on – all of us who had peered into the thick of darkness, death, nothingness. We all go to the office and read engrossing novels.

VIII

The great hammer of war is a terrible thing, but even it is powerless in the face of dull human labor. As long as men live, they work. Death says: I will come to collect you at midnight. But man is busy – with a book, a plow, a machine – and he says, it's only 11, I am alive and I'm working.

A factory near Armentières was buzzing with work. A group of German hussars approached; shots were fired. The women in the factory remained at their stations. Any minute, the building could be hit with an artillery shell, and really, who cares about the batiste they were weaving? Still, they worked. A German officer appeared at the door, shouted:

"Clear out! You could be killed!"

The women answered in unison: "We'll leave when it's time to leave – at six."

* * *

When the French began evacuating Verdun, they ordered the farmers in nearby villages to leave as well. The Germans had already begun shelling the area, but the farmers remained, risking their lives to go about their business. They refused to budge even when ordered to directly.

"You'll die here, then, at your farms!" the authorities warned.

"Haven't died yet, have we? It's a bad time to move anyway – gotta bring in the potatoes..."

* * *

I met an old miller in Picardy. A British artillery unit was positioned right next to his mill. The miller went about his work as if none of it was there: neither the men, nor the German shells that exploded at a hundred paces from them. The only thing he cared about was how to keep the soldiers from wiping their oily hands on his clean flour sacks. And he wanted to know when he could start running his mill again.

IX

Ypres. A wide-open square in front of the ruined arches of the old market. A single statue of a medieval woman that had somehow survived the destruction smiles contemplatively among the gaping holes and charred ceilings. Every five minutes, with a great rumble, another heavy shell falls on the dead city. The residents are long gone, and the soldiers are sitting out the bombardment in basements and deep trenches. In the middle of the square, two British soldiers are engrossed in a conversation about the ruins:

"The marketplace and the court building in Rouen are one of the best examples of Gothic secular architecture in Europe…"

"Indeed! I am very glad I had a chance to see Ypres. I hope I'll be able to visit Rouen as well."

Another shell explodes. The men do not even look up, busy making notes in their pocket-books.

In Amiens, a group of Scottish riflemen, just in from the front-line positions, is studying a monument to a local luminary.

"Excuse me, could you tell us who this monument is for?"

The French soldier expresses his confusion by spitting, then says:

"How'd I know? It's always been here…"

The Scots persist:

"Could you show us how to get to the cathedral? When are visitors permitted there?"

And, having gotten their instructions, they depart, determined in the cold, prickly rain. The French soldier wonders out loud:

"Some strange folk, those! Others come to the rear and go to the cafe, or to the girls, you know? And these just can't wait to find a cathedral or a museum – they just stand there and blabber in their own tongue… I've no idea what they get out of it."

I tell myself that the next time I see a herd of overly curious English tourists with their red-covered Baedeker guides at the doors of the Florence

Baptistery or in the halls of the Louvre, I will remember the Ypres tourists **57**

X

In a small house not far from Senlis there lived the old Abbot Messr. Dolley and his housekeeper M-me Tillaut, who walked with a limp and looked like a witch, but was a caring and kindly woman. Abbot Dolley was at work on the definitive and apparently endless "Life of St. Radegund." Like a medieval monk, he spent years hunting for bits of legend in Latin manuscripts, and retold them with great awe, diligently drawing each letter of his words. His book, if he would ever finish it, stood little chance of being published, and the pages of his manuscript would most probably end up with the shopkeeper next door, who would use them to wrap candles or soap. Sometimes, in the evenings, the old abbot would read from his work to his housekeeper. The good woman would be moved to tears:

"Oh, Monsieur *l'abbé*, she was the saintest of the saints!"

I never laid eyes on this book, and I think it was of no use to anyone except those two old people, who lived quietly, far from the world, and thought the tiny Senlis a noisy and sinful capital. What happened to them? The Prussian army came and accused the abbot of giving shelter to the French partisans.

"Tomorrow at dawn, you will be executed along with the other criminals," they told him. Then they locked him in his own broom closet and left.

At night, the housekeeper peered into the closet through the tiny window.

"Monsieur, these beasts will kill you! Tell me what to do!"

The abbot was overjoyed to see her.

"M-me Tillaut! I thought you'd never make it back here! Please, bring me paper and ink."

"Oh no! Monsieur must wish to compose his will?"

"Not at all! I want to finish chapter sixteen!"

THE FACE OF WAR

XI

There are times when death retreats, powerless in the face of most mundane things. All-powerful, it shrinks before habit or everyday kindness, and almost as often – before a good joke.

* * *

A rock, with a note wrapped around it, flies into the window:

"I will cross the lines tonight – don't shoot. I'm from Alsace. *Vive la France!*"

A man runs in the night. The Germans open fire. He swims, crawls across the river between the lines. He barely makes it, sits there, teeth clattering, can't speak. A French officer orders some rum to be brought. The man shouts:

"No way! I am a member of the Colmar Temperance society! It's a wonderful group, we have two reading rooms, a dining room and four chapters!"

* * *

When Verdun was evacuated in a hurry, the old watchman of the town-hall stayed behind. The Germans bombarded the city with 350-millimeter shells. You know what the old man did? He put up the wedding announcements on the wall of the town-hall, because the law required they be posted two weeks before the ceremony. The responsible parties had long since left town, only the soldiers were left, it was dangerous to go above ground. But the old man went on doing his job.

* * *

Small French towns have a special vocation: the announcer. If someone loses a wallet, or a dog runs loose, the announcer walks the streets, beats on a drum and tells everyone about the accident.

I was in Compiègne not long ago. Shells were falling on the town. A little old man walked down the street with great dignity, beat on a drum, and shouted:

"M-me LeBrui lost a gold pin with three emeralds! Reward to the one who returns it – fifty francs!"

XII

Battlefields of the Marne, two years later. The old wounds have not healed, but they scabbed over. The healing hand of time has touched the torn earth. Here and there stood orphaned buildings in the villages: a ruined farm, a leaning bell-tower, a half-burned barn. The walls are freshly repaired. Grass is growing in the craters left by the artillery shells. And crosses, many crosses, sometimes single and then clustered into small groups. Some have names, others only inscriptions: "Here lie eight French soldiers;" "This is a grave of an unknown soldier."

Hay wagons move down the road. A woman wearing a mourning veil seems to be looking for a particular grave. She has a piece of paper – a letter? a map? – in her hand. She leans, reads the names, walks on. She may not ever find it.

More inscriptions everywhere: "Be respectful of the graves and do not tread on the crops."

These were put up on the farmers' request: so many people came to look for their dead, they were stomping out the new planting. Every grave is nestled in new wheat, it is crowded, life doesn't give death an inch here. Many black-clad women read the farmers' rational plea. I wonder if they thought it a mockery or a piece of ultimate, all-reconciling wisdom.

We're on a hill. A gray-haired old man is telling us about the battle. His delivery is very even, which makes it sound sort of epic, as if the events belonged to a very distant past:

"The Germans came from over there. They built their trenches here. At night on the third day..."

After he's finished with his tale, he asks:

"Do you know, Messr., how much longer before they let us plow over the graves? So much land is going to waste."

At the bottom of the hill, children play; their voices carry far in the pre-dusk quiet. The fields under the early autumn sun are tawny and beautiful. I remember a long time ago, before the war, visiting the fields near Sedan where I stood half-listening (as an indifferent tourist) to the guide's "The Prussian cavalry approached from that direction..."and admiring the golden plumage of aspen trees and swallows diving low to the ground. Here, too, curious travelers will come; here, too, they will listen to explanations, study the monuments and enjoy the rosy, sadness-free sunset.

The veiled woman falls on the ground in front of a cross. Did she find the one she was looking for? Or has she despaired, and kneeled at a nameless grave? She will not forget. Neither will I. Boys shriek at the bottom of the hill. I want to tell them, Play! Grow up! What is all our mourning, and our Great War, and death itself before the unshakeable rights of Life that rules over all?

First published in Russian: 1916
Translation by Nina Shevchuk-Murray

Тише
(«Поэты, не пишите слишком рано...»)
Зинаида Гиппиус

> Громки будут великие дела.
> Федор Сологуб, 7 августа 1914

Поэты, не пишите слишком рано,
Победа ещё в руке Господней.
Сегодня ещё дымятся раны,
Никакие слова не нужны сегодня.

В часы неоправданного страданья
И нерешённой битвы
Нужно целомудрие молчанья
И, может быть, тихие молитвы.

8 августа 1914

Quiet
("Poets, don't write too soon, too boldly...")
Zinaida Gippius

> Loud shall the great deeds be.
> Fyodor Sologub, 7 August 1914

Poets, don't write too soon, too boldly.
Victory is God's to grant.
This very hour wounds still smolder.
No words are needed yet.

Today's unjustified suffering, violence,
a battle not yet won,
call for the chastity of silence –
perhaps a quiet orison.

8 August 1914
Translation by Boris Dralyuk

Петроградское небо мутилось дождём…

Александр Блок

Петроградское небо мутилось дождём,
    На войну уходил эшелон.
Без конца — взвод за взводом и штык за штыком
    Наполнял за вагоном вагон.

В этом поезде тысячью жизней цвели
    Боль разлуки, тревоги любви,
Сила, юность, надежда… В закатной дали
    Были дымные тучи в крови.

И, садясь, запевали *Варяга* одни,
    А другие — не в лад — *Ермака*,
И кричали ура, и шутили они,
    И тихонько крестилась рука.

Вдруг под ветром взлетел опадающий лист,
    Раскачнувшись, фонарь замигал,
И под чёрною тучей весёлый горнист
    Заиграл к отправленью сигнал.

И военною славой заплакал рожок,
    Наполняя тревогой сердца.
Громыханье колёс и охрипший свисток
    Заглушило *ура* без конца.

Уж последние скрылись во мгле буфера,
    И сошла тишина до утра,
А с дождливых полей всё неслось к нам *ура*,
    В грозном клике звучало: *пора!*

Нет, нам не было грустно, нам не было жаль,
    Несмотря на дождливую даль.
Это — ясная, твёрдая, верная сталь,
    И нужна ли ей наша печаль?

Эта жалость — её заглушает пожар,
    Гром орудий и топот коней.
Грусть — ее застилает отравленный пар
    С галицийских кровавых полей…

1 сентября 1914

The Petrograd sky had grown turbid with rain...
Alexander Blok

The Petrograd sky had grown turbid with rain.
    A troop-train was headed to war.
Platoons and platoons — bayonets, bayonets —
    were filling up car after car.

On that train, a full thousand lives were in bloom
    with parting's pain, the torment of love,
strength, youth, hope... In the faraway sunset
    smoky clouds were covered in blood.

Some struck up the "Varyag," some — off-key — the "Yermak,"
    as each found a seat by and by,
and they shouted "Hurrah," and they laughed, and they joked,
    while crossing themselves on the sly.

Then the wind swept up a leaf all of a sudden,
    the lantern winked as it began to sway,
and underneath a pitch-black cloud, a cheerful bugler
    gave the signal — they were on their way.

And the bugle wailed in martial glory,
    filling hearts with torment and alarm.
The rumbling of the wheels and raspy whistle
    were drowned out by an endless "Hurrah!"

The last buffers had already vanished in the darkness,
    and a calm had descended till dawn;
yet we could hear "It's time" in that "Hurrah" that reached us,
    menacing, from fields drenched by the rain.

No, we did not feel sad, did not feel pity,
    despite the rain as far as we could see.
For this was steel – clear, reliable, and sturdy –
    and what use could sorrow be to steel?

This pity — it's drowned out by fire,
    the thud of hooves, and the thunder of guns.
This sadness is veiled by the poisoned mist wafting
    from the bloody Galician plains...

1 September 1914
Translation by Boris Dralyuk

Запасному жена

Фёдор Сологуб

Милый друг мой, сокол ясный!
Едешь ты на бой опасный, –
Помни, помни о жене.
Будь любви моей достоин.
Как отважный, смелый воин
Бейся крепко на войне.
Если ж только из-под пушек
Станешь ты гонять лягушек,
Так такой не нужен мне!

Что уж нам Господь ни судит,
Мне и то утехой будет,
Что жила за молодцом.
В плен врагам не отдавайся,
Умирай иль возвращайся
С гордо поднятым лицом,
Чтоб не стыдно было детям
В час, когда тебя мы встретим,
Называть тебя отцом.

Знаю, будет много горя.
Бабьих слёз прольётся море.
Но о нас ты не жалей.
Бабы русские не слабы, –
Без мужей подымут бабы
Кое-как своих детей.
Обойдёмся понемногу, –
Люди добрые помогут,
Много добрых есть людей.

11 августа 1914 года

A Wife to a Reservist
Fyodor Sologub

My dear friend, my falcon bright!
You're heading to a dangerous fight -
remember me, your loving wife.
Prove worthy of my love, my dear.
Fight mightily when you're at war,
like a hero strong and brave.
If you crawl beneath the guns,
hunting frogs along the ground -
I don't need that kind of knave!

Who knows what God will send our way –
it's a comfort just to say
that my husband was so fine.
Don't fall captive to our foe –
either die or come back home
with your face raised proud and high,
so that when we greet your train,
our little ones are not ashamed
to call you father, meet your eyes.

I know that there'll be lots of grief,
that women's tears will make a sea.
But don't pity us, my dear.
Russian women aren't weaklings –
we'll bring up the little ones
by ourselves, so don't you fear.
Bit by bit, we'll get along –
good folks'll lend a helping hand.
There are lots of good folks here.

August 11, 1914
Translation by Boris Dralyuk

Война

Николай Гумилёв

М. М. Чичагову.

Как собака на цепи тяжёлой,
Тявкает за лесом пулемёт,
И жужжат шрапнели, словно пчёлы,
Собирая ярко-красный мёд.

А «ура» вдали, как будто пенье
Трудный день окончивших жнецов.
Скажешь: это – мирное селенье
В самый благостный из вечеров.

И воистину светло и свято
Дело величавое войны,
Серафимы, ясны и крылаты,
За плечами воинов видны.

Тружеников, медленно идущих
На полях, омоченных в крови,
Подвиг сеющих и славу жнущих,
Ныне, Господи, благослови.

Как у тех, что гнутся над сохою,
Как у тех, что молят и скорбят,
Их сердца горят перед Тобою,
Восковыми свечками горят.

Но тому, о Господи, и силы
И победы царский час даруй,
Кто поверженному скажет: – Милый,
Вот, прими мой братский поцелуй!

1914

War
Nikolai Gumilev

To M. M. Chichagov

A machine gun yelps beyond the trees,
like a dog on a heavy chain,
and shrapnel buzzes, just like bees
collecting bright red honey.

A "Hurrah" sounds from far off, like the singing
of reapers when a hard day's done.
This might seem like the most blessèd evening
in a peaceful little settlement.

And in truth, it is a deed that's bright and holy –
the majestic deed of waging war;
one sees wingèd Seraphim so clearly
behind the shoulders of the fighting men.

I ask Thee now to grant Thy blessing, Lord,
upon laborers, who slowly make their way
across fields that have been soaked with blood –
upon the sowers' feats, the reapers' glory.

Like those who bend above the wooden plough,
like those who pray, like those who mourn,
their hearts burn before Thee now –
like wax candles, their hearts burn.

But I ask Thee, Lord, to grant both strength
and the regal hour of victory to him
who says to the defeated: "My dear friend,
please accept from me a brother's kiss!"

1914
Translation by Boris Dralyuk

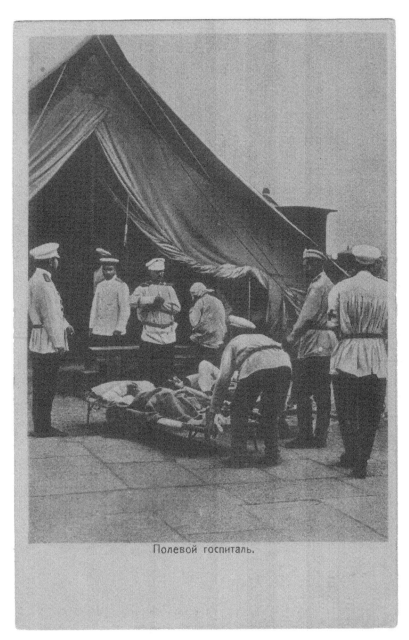

Полевой госпиталь.

Field Hospital
World War I postcard, Gary Bowman Collection, UNC Chapel Hill.

Though he is all but forgotten by most non-Russians, Leonid Andreyev was a major figure of the Silver Age. His prose and drama were influenced both by the realist tradition and by the symbolist movement that followed it. As "The Wounded Soldier" demonstrates, Andreyev's work was also informed by his deep social conscience.

The Wounded Soldier
Leonid Andreyev

A sad and disquieting image often rises before my eyes.

It happened in Petrograd, on the staircase of a large, new building, one apartment of which was transformed into a private ward. When I entered the porter's lodge, on my way to visit a friend, I saw that it was filled with wounded soldiers, who had just arrived, while curious spectators crowded near the plate-glass door. The house was new and luxuriously furnished, and the elevator on which the wounded soldiers were taken up was carefully covered with some kind of cloth, for fear that the velvet would be soiled and the insects would get into the seams. Upstairs the wounded were cordially greeted by a priest and a man dressed in white. After having kissed the priest's hand, the wounded, evidently embarrassed by the bright light and the luxury of the place, entered the ward awkwardly and silently. There were no seriously wounded on stretchers among them, all were able to walk; yet it was painful to look at them.

There was a wounded soldier in one of the last groups taken up by the elevator who strangely attracted everybody's attention. He was a short, young, lean, ghastly pale Jew. All the wounded were pale, but there was something sinister about the pallor of his face; it was a paleness of an utterly exhausted, anæmic or fatally sick man. He was walking alone, feebly moving his feet, and like everybody else bent to kiss the hand of the priest, but he hardly knew what he was doing, and his kiss was strangely indifferent and meaningless. He was evidently wounded in his arm, which he held stretched out. Several fingers were wrapped up; the others, which were not injured, were covered with a crust of dirt and blood. But on his coat, on the back, there was a large brown blotch of blood, a very large one, covering almost half of his back and in the midst of the soft cloth it bulged stiffly as if starched. And this horrible spot told the simple story of the battle and the wound. But it was not the stain that made him so peculiarly conspicuous – other soldiers had similar blotches – it was rather his unusual pallor, thinness and smallness, and, above all, an expression of peculiar timidity, as if he was not at all sure whether his behavior was appropriate and whether he had come to the right place. The faces of the other wounded soldiers, non-Jews, expressed nothing of the kind. These men were confused, but not afraid, and walked straight ahead, into the ward.

And then I recollected how a military sanitarian, whose duty it is to escort a train of wounded soldiers, had told me that the wounded Jews actually try not to moan. It was hardly credible, and at first I did not believe it; how was it possible that a wounded soldier, freshly picked up from the battlefield and lying among wounded soldiers, should try not to moan, as all do? But the sanitarian confirmed his statement and added: they are afraid to attract attention to themselves.

The Jewish soldier entered the ward after the others, and the door was closed, but his image, sorrowful and disquieting, lingered before my eyes. Of course, he, too, tried not to attract attention – and therein is the cause of his shyness; and when his wound will be dressed and he will be put into bed, he will also try not to moan. For, what right has he to moan aloud?

It is very possible that he has no right of settlement in Petrograd and is allowed to stay there only as one of the wounded; a rather precarious right! And that which is home for others is nothing but a kind of honorable imprisonment for him; he will be kept for a while, then they will let him go, saying: "Go away, you must not be here."

And what if his mother, or sister, or father, who also have no right of settlement, will desire to come to him and kiss his bloodstained hand, which has defended Russia – vague, distant Russia? But these reflections and questions came to my mind later. At the moment, I beheld, with the eyes of a peaceful citizen, the bloody, hardened blotch and the dreadful pallor of war, and the needless terror before that which, after all, is your own, and I felt an overwhelming depression and sadness.

First published in Russian: 1917
Translation by Avrahm Yarmolinsky

Газеты

Максимилиан Волошин

Я пробегаю жадным взглядом
Вестей горючих письмена,
Чтоб душу, влажную от сна,
С утра ожечь ползучим ядом.

В строках кровавого листа
Кишат смертельные трихины,
Проникновенны, лезвиины,
Неистребимы, как мечта.

Бродила мщенья, дрожжи гнева,
Вникают в мысль, гниют в сердцах,
Туманят дух, цветут в бойцах
Огнями дьявольского сева.

Ложь заволакивает мозг
Тягучей дрёмой хлороформа
И зыбкой полуправды форма
Течёт и лепится, как воск.

И, гнилостной пронизан дрожью,
Томлюсь и чувствую в тиши,
Как, обезболенному ложью,
Мне вырезают часть души.

Не знать, не слышать и не видеть…
Застыть, как соль… уйти в снега…
Дозволь не разлюбить врага
И брата не возненавидеть!

12 мая 1915
Париж

Newspapers
Maximilian Voloshin

I run my greedy eyes across
the flaming letters of the news –
to burn my soul, still damp from sleep,
with creeping poison upon waking.

The lines that fill the bloody sheet
bristle with lethal trichinella –
as penetrating, razor-sharp,
and indestructible as dreams.

Ferment of vengeance, yeast of anger
seep into thoughts, rot in the heart,
befog the soul, and bloom in soldiers
with fires of the devil's sowing.

Lies muddle and becloud the brain
with chloroform's glutinous slumber,
and half-truth's vacillating form
flows and congeals, like molten wax.

Pierced and soaked through with rotten yeast,
I languish silently and feel
part of my soul being removed
while I'm anesthetized by lies.

Oh, not to know, or hear, or see...
To turn to salt... To hide in snow...
Let me not cease loving my foe
and not begin hating my brother!

12 May 1915, Paris
Translation by Boris Dralyuk

"Volunteers for the Front"
Capt. Donald C. Thompson (1917)

By 1918, several million Russian soldiers had been held as prisoners of war in Germany and Austria-Hungary, usually in dreadful conditions. The Soviet-Jewish author Kirill Levin was one of them; he revisited his experiences in both memoirs and fiction throughout the 1920s and 1930s, taking a distinctly Soviet perspective – which, at that time, accommodated pacifist and internationalist vies.

The Wild Battalion
Kirill Levin

I

The train drew in slowly, as if unwillingly, and halted before it had reached the station. From the cars poured soldiers – a mixture of Russians and Austrians – with rifles at the ready.

The stationmaster was upset, but he hid his alarm and went off to find the commander of the battalion. But he could find no commander.

"We're all colonels here," said a soldier with high cheekbones and a low forehead, who looked not at the stationmaster's face but at his shoulders, at the glittering gold of his epaulettes (the front epaulettes were of cloth, were quiet and discreet). Others standing around looked at the epaulettes in the same unfriendly fashion.

Not finding the commander, the stationmaster went away. As he went, feeling uneasily the glances of the soldiers that were prickling his retreating spine, he thought:

"I don't know… I've got no orders… I won't let them get away… sons of bitches… deserters."

But just half an hour later there appeared in the stationmaster's room six soldiers. Four Russians and two Austrians entered noisily with rifles in hand and caps still on their heads. One of them, a fellow with high cheek bones and a low forehead, with extravagantly wide shoulders and calm grey eyes, asked the stationmaster to dispatch their train more quickly. The stationmaster, restraining himself, said that without papers he could not dispatch the train; he asked whence the battalion came from and whither it was going. The high cheek-boned soldier, lightly tapping the floor with his rifle butt and looking the stationmaster in the eyes, answered that those at the front had forgotten about office regulations, they had no papers at all and were in a great hurry. It was necessary to dispatch the battalion quickly.

"Can't," said the stationmaster gloomily. And glaring at the soldier, he added:

"At the front they're fighting... but you willfully..."

"Anybody that wants fighting can have it," slowly answered the soldier, "but we want peace. Fight if you want to. We don't..."

The stationmaster ground his yellow, horse-like teeth, convulsively moving his sharp jowl, and then suddenly went into the rear room, banging the door behind him. The soldier turned to his mates. A swarthy Magyar in Austrian uniform laughed, winking at the door through which the stationmaster had passed, repeating "*Nem sabat.*" A soldier with a scar on his neck pushed forward and said:

"The hardest thing was to leave the front. Well we left. We decided not to fight any more – and we won't. We're fed up with fighting. Let the officers go over the top themselves. We've got other things to do. We'll commandeer an engine and go. That's all."

He went to the exit with a decisive step. He had calm grey eyes; his movements were not hurried. The rest silently followed him. The last to leave was the high-cheekboned soldier, who scratched his bayonet with a finger nail as he went.

They went up the lines to the S.82, a huge and shapely locomotive with a long, tight cylinder, like a bloodhound's belly, sharpened at the front, huge wheels the height of a man, and a short, squat, chopped-off, energetic funnel.

The high-cheekboned soldier struck the iron step of the locomotive with his rifle butt, and, poking his head up, cried: "Hey, anybody there?"

There was no reply, so he fired into the air.

Then in the oval window above there appeared a thin, whiskered face, begrimed and with sunken eyes. The driver asked without haste:

"What are you firing for? Got a lot of cartridges? I'll buy some."

"Drive for our battalion ... we want to go home," replied the soldier, with a threat and a plea in his voice.

And two who were standing at the back – little, thin, yellow fellows – cried in unison, like as two peas: "Uncouple the engine and drive it to our battalion on the third line."

And simultaneously, like winter wolves, spitefully, timid, desperate and worn out with suffering, they snapped back the bolts of their rifles with an accustomed movement. The driver answered:

"I won't uncouple the engine. Ask the boss for an engine for your train."

Two soldiers began climbing up on to the engine; the driver watched them languidly and disdainfully, for he was used to this sort of thing; he had been working for three months on the most disturbed line, the south-western. Then he turned round and stretched out his hand; the sharp, high scream of the siren soared up.

They hauled him down to the ground, and surrounded him, with a ring of bayonets at his chest, but he stood there wearily as if tired of standing and, getting *mahorka*[1] out of his pocket, rolled a cigarette with deep indifference to what was happening around him. Finding that he had no matches, he stretched out his hand to the soldiers and said:

"Give me a light."

The grey-eyed soldier gave him a match and the two little fellows who were as alike as two peas took the bayonets away and began to beg him take them home.

----

1. Tobacco substitute.

The driver looked at the rails, at the signals which for a whole week had been closed, slowly took off his cap – time had traced indelible silver on his head – and suddenly, with a laugh, said:

"Well, seeing it's you ... I'll take your battalion."

II

Three men ran from the station building: the station foreman, a stout fellow in a red cap who had rolling eyes and a big belly; the stationmaster, who was freckled all over and had curved legs, and a third in polished high boots, who looked like a telegraphist. They ran to the third line where, clanking over the iron points, with its still sleepy wheels turning slowly, the S.82 was drawing a long, brick-red line of cars with open doors, from which protruded feet in puttees, high boots, boots, felt boots, slippers and feet that were just plain naked. Seeing the men running toward them, hundreds of soldiers began to bawl and a few shots were fired.

The station foreman stopped at once; the telegraphist, dodging to one side at right angles, stumbled over the rails; he yelled and the stout one, in a panic, yelled too. Then the telegraphist got in behind the linesman's hut and hid himself, all that was visible of him being part of his jacket. The stationmaster squatted down, feeling for his revolver and followed the train with his eyes. The train went ever faster, to the accompaniment of bandit-like screams from the siren. The engine disappeared behind the water tower and only then, tearing off his belt, did the stationmaster seize his revolver and begin to fire at the last car. And when the last bullet had whined past the funnel, he got up, covered with dust, sighed with satisfaction and went off, evil and prickly, champing his sharp jowl.

But the S.82, pulling out into the distance along the endless rails, gave itself, as it were, a shaking up and bounded forward, acquiring with speed a new suppleness, sweep and beauty; its wheels flashed and it breathed with happy strength. And it was surprising and strange to see that from its black, smoky funnel there flew out white, clean clouds of steam.

The wheels squealed, the soldiers sang songs, and trees and meadows retreated behind the train. But on the fields there were no cattle and from the cabins there came no signalmen with the green flags to welcome the train.

Leaning out, the driver watched how at the stations silly little figures cried something in alarm and waved hands and flags. He only gave alarming whistles and the engine hurried forward ever more quickly, cutting the air with its sharp breast.

III

A telegram along the line :

"Stop battalion fleeing from the front. In the battalion are Austrians who fraternized with Russians at the front. Separate them when arrested. . . ."

Military trains had not been running for several days.

Towards evening a wounded officer arrived at the station on a motor trolley. He was worn out, scared and confused, but automatically tried to journey further; when he learned that it was impossible to go any further, he lost heart and let himself be carried away. In the stationmaster's office, having eaten, he revived and presented himself:

"Losev, sub-lieutenant, opera singer."

And then, probably remembering something terrible he whispered:

"They've ceased to listen… A revolt of unheard of dimensions, a universal revolt. The front has collapsed…" and whimperingly he added: "They run away home… they're fed up with the war… They have no use for victory and the fatherland."

Telegraphic communications ceased for some hours, then resumed. They said that one of the stations had been seized by rebellious soldiers, who had pillaged it and then gone off into the forest. Confusion reigned up and down the line.

At night, without any reference to the timetable and without even a signaled warning, a military train arrived. In the darkness, the soldiers sang

Stenka Razin and the familiar song seemed threatening, piratical, full of a new meaning.

And in the night the train left.

In the morning an armored train arrived from the front. The commander of the train questioned the stationmaster for a long time about the Russian-Austrian battalion, sent off a telegram to the whole line about the halting of the battalion and announced that he would start off in an hour.

IV

With each station the danger grew.

All these stationmasters in red caps, and all these people in epaulettes and cockades who skulked in the rear rooms of stations did not inspire the soldiers with confidence.

But at a station where the train arrived at mid-day on the following day, the stationmaster did not delay them, was obliging and polite and himself helped to send the train off quickly. Suspecting a trick, the soldiers constantly followed him around, but he was imperturbable and calm; only when the battalion had departed did he sigh, cross himself and hurry to the telegraph to warn the next station where in the forest, on a side line, in ambush for the battalion, a hidden armored train waited.

In the soldiers' train, which was going ever faster, the high-cheekboned soldier, sitting on a wide board seat, threw out words, as if into the air.

"There's something the matter all the same... I'm worried. I'm afraid of these stations."

The other soldier, with a scar on his neck, standing with his legs wide apart, like a sailor when a ship is rolling, waved a long, clutching hand and glancing at his comrades with calm grey eyes, answered:

"I've thought about it already. I know. We've got to go on further."

He added in the same quiet, confident voice, as though agreeing with something that could not be disputed: "We won't surrender alive."

In the forest, on a signal from the first car, at a point two *versts* from the station, the train stopped. The soldiers poured out into a large clearing, Austrians mingled with Russians. All alike had worried, dark, weather-beaten faces, a tense glitter in their eyes; all were united by a common hatred of war. The first to speak was the soldier with high cheek-bones.

"Comrades, you know how it has been till now," he said, looking round at the crowd. "We left the front, so as not to fight any more, and now they are hunting us. Decide what to do now. Shall we fight or shall we fight against fighting?"

The second speaker was the grey-eyed fellow. He spoke from the crowd, smoking and not leaving his place. His words fell weightily.

"We know how things will be," he began. "We left the front. We won't go back. We've had enough of rotting off. Let them try to take us. We'll break through. We've got to. Isn't that right, comrades?"

They supported him with shouts, curses and complaints about what they had suffered. They would not go back to the front. They would go forward, even if they had to fight. Before the shouts died down, the grey-eyed fellow looked at the crowd with a kind of happy sadness, and, stroking his tobacco-stained whiskers, shouted: "Into the cars."

And giving the soldier with high cheekbones his unfinished cigarette, he went into his car, leaving a brave scent of *mahorka* behind him.

"That's what they're like, the Bolsheviks," shouted some one. "When they start something, they don't give up. Workers..."

V

This station was like any other on the southwestern line; built of brick, with a hexagonal watertower, also of brick. It had a three-wheeled, latticed luggage barrow standing abandoned on the platform, and peasants sleeping with bundles under their heads at the fence.

A few minutes after the train arrived at the station, the armored train, with a muffled rumble of wheels, came out of the forest and drew up opposite the soldiers' train. At once on the gang-boards of the armored train machine guns were run out; low and fat like bull-dogs, they pointed at the train; hundreds of swarthy, hook-nosed men with rifles and hand grenades

– it was difficult to make out where they had come from – surrounded the train.

A tall officer in a Caucasian jacket and Caucasian soft shoes, waving a revolver, ran down the platform and shouted:

"Stay where you are, or we'll fire."

As if to confirm his words, a three-incher spoke from the armored train and a shell soared high in the air. The officer ran to the engine which was being uncoupled in a very unskillful way by hook-nosed soldiers who were laughingly watched by the driver. And when, finally, they uncoupled it, and the officer shouted "Off!", the driver, paying no attention to the soldiers standing near the boiler, moved a lever and the engine, its wheels rumbling, turned over the points into the sidings.

The train stood like a man without a head. In the first car were the delegates. The soldier with high cheekbones looked through the window, hiding the grey-eyed fellow with his chin on the muzzle of his rifle and reflected; the two little red-haired fellows looked at the man with high cheekbones, then at the grey-eyed man with an expression of readiness on their faces. A Magyar excitedly said something to a Czech, but the latter, biting a black pipe, did not reply. The high-cheekboned man left the window and, going up to the grey-eyed man, asked what they should do. The latter lifted his rifle, took the bolt and with a skilful motion of a thick finger loaded the magazine with all his five cartridges. The high-cheekboned man looked at him for a second and this second was enough; he remembered the trenches, the long, cold nights, remembered that in any case he had nothing to lose, and grasped his own rifle which had been standing in the corner.

The Magyar was the first to jump out and run the length of the train to his mates. With his rifle on his shoulders, the grey-eyed one ran after him, and taking no notice of the bullets which were already falling, shouted at the top of his voice:

"Out of the cars, rapid fire," and with both hands tearing the "lemons" (hand grenades) from his belt, he hurled them one after the other into the garden, over the platform fence, into the squad of hook-nosed soldiers.

The whiskered and white-teethed Magyars were advancing in a wide line. The man with high cheekbones ran under fire along the train, opening carriage doors where they were closed and shouting: "Forward… fight… hurrah…" Some crouched in the corners of the carriages, but most jumped out on to the platform, just like potatoes bursting out of a bag, firing as they leapt and shouting to keep their spirits up.

The grey-eyed soldier, powerful and dogged, the veins of his neck swelling, shouted above the sound of the firing:

"Beat those priggish officers, down with war… hurrah!"

The Magyars attacked with songs on their lips. Only the refrain of *Eizhuzhika* was heard. The Russians went forward with shouts and oaths when the first shrapnel from the armored train broke on the platform and the ferociously indifferent machine-guns beat down a whole line with their fire. The Magyar delegate fell heavily on the luggage barrow, and, struggling to escape, hung with his head down. Soldiers ran to all points, creeping under wheels and hiding behind cars. One who had gone mad from fear rang furiously on the station alarm bell. At the entrance to the third-class waiting room the little red-haired delegates lay, one on his side in contortions, the other flung backwards, with his head on his comrade's stomach.

Through the window of the ladies' lavatory, the grey-eyed man and three others jumped into the backyard of the station, firing as they ran.

Right behind the semi-circular fence, the forest began and, breathing heavily, with blood streaming from them, they ran silently into the forest, like hunted animals, feeling elemental hatred towards those who had sent them to war: blind, not yet conscious indignation. Within them hid the embryo of a great revolt, preparing the war against war.

1918
Translator unknown

Без оправданья
Зинаида Гиппиус

Нет, никогда не примирюсь.
 Верны мои проклятья.
Я не прощу, я не сорвусь
 В железные объятья.

Как все, пойду, умру, убью,
 Как все – себя разрушу,
Но оправданием – свою
 Не запятнаю душу.

В последний час, во тьме, в огне,
 Пусть сердце не забудет:
Нет оправдания войне!
 И никогда не будет.

И если это Божья длань –
 Кровавая дорога –
Мой дух пойдет и с Ним на брань,
 Восстанет и на Бога.

        Апрель 1916, Санкт-петербург

Without Justification
Zinaida Gippius

No, I will never make my peace.
 There's truth in all my curses.
I won't forgive, won't throw myself
 into iron and steel embraces.

Like everyone, I'll die, I'll kill –
 ruin myself, like everyone –
but I refuse to stain my soul
 by justifying what goes on.

When death is near, in darkness, fire,
 let my heart not forget:
One cannot justify the war!
 One can't, one simply can't.

And if this is God's Hand at work –
 this awful, bloody road –
my spirit will not shrink or shirk,
 but rise against the Lord.

April 1916, St. Petersburg
Translation by Boris Dralyuk

„ Не везетъ же! Ну и бабы!" - Негодуютъ эти швабы.

"No luck! These women are a pain!" the angry Swabians complain.
World War I postcard, Gary Bowman Collection, UNC Chapel Hill

Mikhail Zoshchenko, who would go on to make his name as the leading Soviet satirist of the 1920s, was a highly decorated officer in the Imperial Army. He was wounded and gassed at the front, suffering ill health for the rest of his life. The jaundiced view of human nature expressed in his satirical stories may have been innate or shaped in childhood, but it was surely influenced by his experiences during the war.

Before Sunrise
Mikhail Zoshchenko

FOREWORD

I conceived this book a very long time ago. Immediately after I brought out my *Youth Restored*.

For almost ten years I collected materials for this new book and waited for a calm year to sit down and work in the quiet of my study.

But this did not happen.

On the contrary. German bombs fell twice near my materials. The portfolio containing my manuscripts was littered with lime and bricks. The burning flames licked them. And I am surprised that they escaped without damage.

The collected material flew with me in an airplane across the German front, out of besieged Leningrad.

I took twenty heavy notebooks with me. To lessen their weight I tore off their calico bindings. And still they weighed close to eight kilograms of the twelve kilograms of baggage allowed on the airplane. And there was a moment when I sorely grieved for having taken this rubbish with me instead of warm underpants and an extra pair of boots.

But the love of literature triumphed. I resigned.

Now she almost never left my room.

It's a good thing the world war began soon after. I left.

1915-1917

Fate treated me more kindly
Than a multitude of others...

Twelve Days

I'm riding from Vyatka to Kazan to get reinforcements for my regiment. Riding with post-horses. There's no other connection. I'm riding in a *kibitka*, wrapped in a blanket and fur coats.

Three horses race over the snow. Desolate all around. A fierce frost.

Beside me sits Ensign S. We're riding together for reinforcements.

It's the second day we've been riding. All the words have been said. All the recollections repeated. We're bored like mad.

Taking the revolver from his holster, Ensign S. shoots at the white insulators on the telegraph poles.

These shots irritate me. I get mad at Ensign S. I say to him gruffly: "Cut it out... you bonehead!"

I expect an uproar, a shout. But instead of this I hear a plaintive voice in reply. He says:

"Ensign Zoshchenko... no need to stop me. Let me do what I want. I'll arrive at the front and get killed."

I gaze at his upturned nose, I look into his pitiful bluish eyes. I recall his face after almost thirty years. He actually was killed on the second day after he took his position. In that war ensigns lived on average no more than twelve days.

Feeling Sleepy

We enter a ballroom. At the windows, raspberry velvet curtains. In between, mirrors in golden frames.

A waltz is booming. It's played on the piano by a man in tuxedo. An aster in his buttonhole. But the mug on him – it's that of a murderer.

On the sofas and armchairs sit officers and ladies. Several couples dance.

A drunken cornet enters. Sings: "The Austrians are stupid men, if war with Russia they begin…"

Everyone takes up the song. They laugh.

I sit down on the sofa. Beside me, a woman. She's about thirty years old. A bit plump. Dark. Merry.

Glancing into my eyes, she says: "Shall we dance?"

I sit somber, morose. Shake my head no.

"Feeling sleepy?" she asks. "Then come to my place."

We go to her room. In the room, a Chinese lantern. Chinese screens. Chinese robes. It's amusing. Funny.

We go to bed.

It's already twelve. My eyelids grow heavy. But I can't fall asleep. Feel bad. Miserable. Uneasy. I'm weary.

She's bored with me. She tosses, sighs. Reaches over to my shoulder. Says:

"Don't get angry if I go to the ballroom for a short while. They're playing lotto there now. They're dancing."

"As you wish," I say.

She kisses me gratefully and leaves. I fall asleep immediately. Toward morning she's not there, and I again shut my eyes.

A bit later she is sleeping peacefully, and I, dressing quietly, leave.

The First Night

I enter the hut. On the table, a kerosene lamp. The officers are playing cards. On an army cot, puffing on a pipe, sits the lieutenant-colonel.

I salute.

"At ease," says the lieutenant-colonel. And turning to the players, he nearly yells: "Lieutenant K. Eight o'clock. Time for you to go to work."

The crafty-looking lieutenant, handsome, with thin moustaches, dealing the cards, answers:

"Yes, sir, Pavel Nikolaevich... At once... As soon as I finish this hand."

I gaze rapturously at the lieutenant. In a moment he has to go to work – into the night, into the darkness, on a scouting party, to the rear. Maybe he'll be killed, wounded. But he answers so easily, so gaily and jokingly.

Looking over some papers, the lieutenant-colonel says to me:

"Take a rest for now, but tomorrow we'll send you 'to work' too."

"Yes, sir," I answer.

The lieutenant goes out. The officers go to bed. Quiet. I listen to the distant gunshots. This is my first night near the front. No sleeping for me.

Toward morning Lieutenant K. returns. He's dirty, tired.

I ask him sympathetically:

"Not wounded?"

The lieutenant shrugs his shoulders. I say:

"I also have a spot of 'work' ahead of me today."

Smiling, the lieutenant says:

"What do you think, that I went out on a military operation? I went to work with the battalion. Three kilometers from here, to the rear. We're fortifying the second line there."

I'm horribly uncomfortable, ashamed. I come close to crying in my vexation.

But the lieutenant is already snoring.

Nerves

Two soldiers are cutting up a pig. The pig squeals so badly you can't stand it. I go closer.

One soldier is sitting on the pig. The hand of the other, armed with a knife, skillfully slits open the belly. White lard of immeasurable thickness spreads out on both sides.

The squeal is so bad it's time to stop up your ears.

"Hey, fellows," I say, "you could have stunned it, shut it up with something. What's the point of slicing it up that way?"

"Can't be helped, your honor," says the soldier sitting on the pig. "You won't get the same taste."

Catching sight of my silver sabre and the emblem on my epaulets, the soldier leaps up. The pig shoots out.

"Sit, sit," I say. "Finish it up already."

"Quick isn't good either," says the solider with the knife. "Too much quickness spoils the fat."

Looking at me with sympathy, the first soldier says: "It's war, your honor! People are moaning. And you feel sorry for a pig."

Making the final gesture with the knife, the second soldier says:

"His honor has a case of nerves."

The conversation is taking on a familiar tone. This isn't proper. I want to leave, but I don't leave.

The first soldier says:

"In the Augustowo forest the bone was shattered on this hand here. Went right to the table. A half-glass of spirits. They start cutting. And I have a bite of sausage."

"And it didn't hurt?"

"How could it not hurt? It hurt most excessively... I ate the sausage. Give me, I say, some cheese. I had just eaten up the cheese when the surgeon says: Finished, let's sew it up. My pleasure, I say... Now you, your honor, you wouldn't have been able to stand it."

"His honor has weak nerves," the second soldier says again.

I leave.

An Attack

Exactly at midnight we leave the entrenchments. It's very dark. I hold a revolver. "Softly, softly," I whisper, "don't bang your canteens."

But it's impossible to get rid of the rattling.

The Germans open fire. How vexing. That means they've noticed our maneuver.

Amid the whistling and screeching of bullets, we rush forward to drive the Germans out of their trenches.

A hurricane of fire swells up. Machine guns, rifles are firing. And the artillery enters the affair.

Men are falling around me. I feel a bullet has singed my leg. But I rush forward.

Now we're right at the German obstructions. My grenadiers cut the wire.

Furious machine-gun fire cuts short our work. It's impossible to raise your hand. We lie still.

We lie an hour, maybe two.

Finally the telephone man extends the telephone receiver to me. It's the battalion commander speaking:

"Retreat to your former positions."

I pass the order down the line.

We crawl back.

Next morning they bandage me up in the regimental infirmary. A minor wound. And not made by a bullet, but by a shell fragment.

The regimental commander, Prince Makayev, tells me:

"I'm very pleased with your company."

"We didn't do anything, your excellency," I answer in some confusion.

"You did what was demanded of you. You see, it was a diversion and not an assault."

"Ah, it was a diversion?"

"It was simply a diversion. We had to draw the foe from the left flank. That's the place where the assault was."

In my heart I feel unbelievable vexation, but I don't let on.

In the Garden

In front of the balcony of a dacha there is a beautiful flowerbed with a yellow glass ball on a stand.

They bring the dead in carts and lay them out in the grass alongside this flowerbed.

They lay them out like logs, one next to the other.

They lie there yellow and motionless, like wax dolls.

Removing the glass ball from the stand, the grenadiers dig a grave for their brothers.

By the porch stand the regimental commander and the staff officers. The regimental priest walks up.

Quiet. Somewhere far off, the artillery is bellowing.

The dead are lowered into the pit on towels.

The priest walks around and pronounces the words of the last rites. We hold our hands up in salute.

They batter down the grave with their feet. Erect a cross.

Unexpectedly, another cartload of dead rolls up.

The regimental commander says:

"Well, how can this be, men. It should all be done together."

A Feldwebel,[1] arriving on a cart, reports:

"We didn't find them all at first, your excellency. These were on the left side, in a hollow."

"What can we do?" says the commander.

"Permit me to append, your excellency," says the Feldwebel, "why not just let 'em lie a bit. Maybe tomorrow ther'll be some more. And then we can bury 'em all together."

The commander agrees. The dead are carried off to the barn.

We go to dinner.

The Regiment in a Pocket

The regiment spreads out over the highway. The soldiers are exhausted, tired. For the second day, almost without resting, we have been marching across the fields of Galicia.

---

1. The lowest ranking German non-commissioned officer.

We are retreating. We have no shells.

The regimental commander orders us to sing songs.

The machine gunners, prancing on their horses, strike up *Over the Blue Waves of the Ocean.*

From all sides we hear shots, explosions. The impression is that we are in a pocket.

We march through a village. The soldiers run up to the cottages. We have an order to destroy everything along the highway.

It's a dead village. No pity for it. There's not a soul here. There's not even any dogs. Not even a single chicken, which usually are found in abandoned villages.

The grenadiers run up to the little cottages and set fire to the straw roofs. Smoke rises up to the sky.

And suddenly, in an instant, the dead village comes alive. Women, children go running. Men appear. Cows moo. Horses neigh. We hear shouts, crying and screeching.

I see how one soldier, having just lit a roof, beats it out in his confusion with his cap.

I turn away. We march on.

We march until evening. And we march at night. All around, the red glow of fires. Shots. Explosions.

Toward morning the regimental commander says:

"Now I can say it. For two days our regiment has been in a pocket. Tonight we came out of it."

We drop on the grass and immediately fall asleep.

Breakthrough

I memorized the name of this village: Tuchla.

We hastily dug out some trenches here. But we hadn't time to string up the obstructions. The barbed wire lay behind us in big rolls.

In the evening I receive an order – report to headquarters. Amid the whistling of bullets I go there with my orderly sergeant.

I enter the dugout of regiment headquarters.

The regimental commander, smiling, says to me:

"Lad, stay here with the staff. The adjutant will be getting a battalion. You'll take this place."

I lie down to sleep in a low hut. Take off my boots for the first time in a week.

In the early morning I am awakened by a burst of shells. I run out of the hut.

The regimental commander and the staff officers are standing beside saddled horses. I see they are all agitated and even shaken. Shells fall around us, fragments hiss and trees crash down. Nevertheless, the officers stand motionless, stonelike.

The chief signal officer, biting out his words, says to me:

"The regiment is surrounded and taken captive. In about twenty minutes the Germans will be here... There's no link with division headquarters... The front is broken up for six kilometers."

Nervously tugging op his gray sidewhiskers, the regimental commander shouts at me:

"Quick, ride to division headquarters. Ask what are the directives. Tell them we headed for supplies, where our reserve battalion is waiting..."

Jumping on a horse, I dash down a forest road together with an orderly.

Early morning. The sun gilds a meadow, visible to my right.

I ride out into the meadow. I want to see what is happening and where the Germans are. I want to get a complete picture of the breakthrough.

I jump off the horse and walk up to the top of a knoll.

I am all aglitter in the sun – with my sabre, epaulets and binoculars, which I put to my eyes. I see some distant columns and the German artillery on horseback. I shrug my shoulders. It's very far away.

Suddenly, a shot. One, two, three. Three-inch shells land beside me. I hardly have time to lie down.

And, lying there, I see a German battery below the knoll. No more than a thousand paces away.

Again shots. And now the shrapnel explodes above me.

The orderly waves his hand at me. With his other hand he points to the road below where a battalion of Germans is moving.

I jump on my horse. And we dash away.

I Came for Nothing

I ride up to the high gates at a gallop. This is division headquarters.

I'm excited and agitated. The collar of my field jacket hangs open, The cap sits on the back of my head.

Jumping off my horse, I go through a wicket gate,

A staff officer, Lieutenant Zradlovsky, comes directly up to me. He hisses through his teeth:

"Looking like that... Button up your collar."

I button my collar and adjust my cap.

The staff officers are standing beside saddled horses.

Among them I see the division commander, General Gabayev, and the chief of staff, Lieutenant Shaposhnikov.

I make my report.

"I know," the general says irritably.

"What should I relay to my commander, your eminence?"

"Relay that..."

I sense some sort of curse on the general's tongue, but he holds it back.

The officers glance at each other. The chief of staff almost laughs out loud.

"Relay that... Well, what can I relay to a man who has lost his regiment... You came for nothing..." I walk away in confusion.

I gallop off on my horse again. And suddenly I see my regimental commander. He's tall, lean. His cap's in his hand. The wind ruffles his gray sidewhiskers. He stands in the field and halts the departing soldiers. These are not soldiers from our regiment. The commander runs up to each one shouting and entreating.

The soldiers obediently go to the edge of the forest. There I see our reserve battalion and some two-wheeled supply wagons.

I go up to the officers. The commander also comes up to them. He mutters:

"My glorious Mingrelsy Regiment is lost." Throwing his cap on the ground, he stomps on it in a rage.

We console him. We say that five hundred of us have remained. That's no small number. We'll have a regiment again.

Hell

We're sitting in some sort of kiln. It's seven hundred paces to the trenches. Bullets are whistling. And shells blow up nearby. But regimental commander Balo Makayev is joyful, almost gay. We have a regiment again – a hastily reinforced battalion.

For three days and nights we have sustained the assault of the Germans without retreating.

"Write," the commander dictates to me. On my field stachel lies a notebook. I write a communique to division headquarters.

A heavy shell explodes ten paces from the kiln. We are sprayed with trash, filth, straw.

Through the smoke and dust I see the commander's smiling face.

"It's nothing," he says, "keep writing."

I take up my writing again. My pencil literally jumps up and down from the nearby explosions. Across the yard from us the house is burning. Again a heavy shell explodes with a horrible rumble. This one was right beside us. The fragments go flying – squealing and moaning. For some reason I stick a little burning fragment in my pocket.

There's no need to sit in this kiln, which doesn't even have a roof on it.

"Your excellency," I say, "it would be more reasonable to transfer to the forward line."

"We stay here," the commander says stubbornly.

A hurricane of artillery fire descends on the village. The air is filled with moaning, howling, squealing and screeching. It seems to me I have fallen into hell.

It seemed to me I was in hell! Twenty-five years later, I was in hell when a German bomb weighing a ton and a half exploded next door.

I Go On Leave

I have a suitcase in hand. I'm standing in the station "Zalesye." In a moment the train will pull up and I'll return to Petrograd via "Minsk" and "Dno."

The coaches pull up. They are all heated freight cars, with one passenger car. Everyone rushes to the train.

Suddenly, shots. By their sound: ack-acks. German planes appear in the sky. Three of them. They begin to circle around the station. The soldiers shoot at them haphazardly with their rifles.

Two bombs fall from the planes with an oppressive howl and explode near the station.

We all run into the field. In the field there are vegetable gardens, a hospital unit with a red cross on its roof and, farther off, fences of some kind.

I lie down on the ground by a fence.

Having circled the station and dropped another bomb, the planes set their sights on the hospital. Three bombs fall almost simultaneously by the fences, throwing up the earth. This is really swinish. There's a huge cross on the roof. You can't fail to notice it.

Three more bombs. I see how they break away from the planes. I see the beginning of their fall. And then, only the howling and whistling of air.

Our ack-acks fire again. Now the fragments and jackets of our shrapnel spray the field. I press against the fence. And through a chink I see an artillery dump.

Hundreds of cases of artillery shells stand under the open sky.

A watchman sits on the cases, eyeing the planes.

I rise up slowly and peel my eyes for a place to hide. But there's no place. One bomb in the cases, and everything will be turned upside down for several kilometers. After dropping a few more bombs, the planes leave.

I walk slowly back to the train and give my heartfelt blessing to inaccurate shooting. War will become absurd, I think, when technology achieves perfect aim. This year I would have been killed at least forty times.

I Love

I ring. Nadya V. opens the door. She cries out in surprise. And throws her arms around my neck.

On the threshold stand her sisters and mama.

We go out on the street to talk without disturbance. We sit down on a bench at the *Steregushchy* monument.

Squeezing my hands, Nadya weeps. Through tears she says:

"How stupid. Why didn't you write me anything. Why did you leave so unexpectedly. Now a year has passed. I'm getting married."

"Do you love him?" I ask, without yet knowing who he is.

"No, I don't love him. I love you. And I'll never love anyone else. I'll turn him down."

She weeps again. And I kiss her face, wet with the tears.

"But how can I turn him down," says Nadya, interrupting herself in reflection. "We've already exchanged rings. And we've announced our engagement. On that day he gave me an estate in the province of Smolensk."

"Then don't," I say. "After all, I'm going back to the front. And so why should you wait for me? I may be killed or wounded."

Nadya says:

"I'll think everything over. I'll decide myself. You don't have to say anything to me... I'll give you an answer day after tomorrow."

The next day I meet Nadya on the street. She is walking arm in arm with her fiancé.

There's nothing special about this. It's natural. But I'm infuriated.

In the evening I send Nadya a note saying that I've been called immediately back to the front. And a day later I leave.

This was the most stupid and senseless act of my life.

I loved her very much. And this love has not left me to the present day.

Come Tomorrow

At the entrance I meet Tata T. She's so beautiful and so dazzling, that I turn my eyes away from her as from the sun.

She laughs on seeing me. She looks over my uniform with curiosity and touches my silver sabre. Then she says I've really grown up and it's even improper for people to see us together. There would surely be gossip.

We go up the stairs.

Clicking my spurs, I enter her apartment.

At the mirror, Tata adjusts her hairdo. I go over to her and embrace her. She laughs. She's surprised that I've become so bold. She embraces me the way she once did on the stairway.

We kiss. And in comparison to this the whole world strikes me as negligible. And she also doesn't care what's going on around us.

Then she looks at the clock and cries out in terror. Says:

"My husband will be home in a moment."

At that very minute the door opens, and her husband comes in.

Tata barely has time to adjust her hairdo.

The husband sits down in an armchair and looks at us silently.

Tata, not losing her composure, says:

"Nikolai, just take a look at him, how he's changed. Why, just this minute he arrived from the front."

With a sour smile, the husband looks at me.

The conversation doesn't catch on. And I leave with a ceremonious bow. Tata sees me out.

Opening the door to the stairway, she whispers to me:

"Come tomorrow afternoon. He leaves at eleven."

I nod my head silently.

The husband's face and his sour smile stick in my head all day. It strikes me as horrible – and even criminal – to go to her tomorrow afternoon.

In the morning I send Tata a note saying that I must leave immediately for the front.

That evening I go to Moscow and, after spending a few days there, return to my regiment.

The Thief

I'm the battalion commander. I'm upset that discipline is becoming lax among my men.

My grenadiers salute me with a smile. They almost wink at me. Probably I myself am to blame. I converse with them too much. People hang about my dugout all day. For some I have to write letters. Others come for advice.

What advice can I give when I hear them calling me "kiddie" behind my back.

It's come to the point where things have begun to disappear from my dugout. A pipe is missing. A shaving mirror. Candy, paper disappears.

I'll have to shake them up and be hard on them.

We're off duty. I'm sleeping in a cottage, on a bed.

In my sleep I suddenly feel someone's hand stretching across me to the table. I shudder in horror and wake up.

Some damn soldier springs headlong out of the cottage.

I run after him with a revolver in my hand. I am infuriated as never before in my life. I shout: "Halt." And had he not stopped I would have shot him. But he stopped.

I walk up to him. And he suddenly falls to his knees. In his hands he holds my safety razor in a nickel-plated box.

"What did you take it for?" I ask him.

"For *makhorka*, your honor," he mumbles.

I understand that he should be punished, turned over for court-martial. But I lack the strength to do it. I see his dejected face, pitiful smile, trembling hands. It disgusts me that I chased him.

Removing the razor, I hand the box over to him. And walk away, irritated with myself.

July the Twentieth

I stand in the trenches and look with curiosity at the ruins of the little town. This is Smorgon. The right wing of our regiment has dug in beside the vegetable gardens of Smorgon.

This is a famous town, the place from which Napoleon fled, leaving Murat in command.

It's growing dark. I return to my dugout.

A sultry July night. Taking off my field jacket, I write letters.

It's nearly one o'clock already. Ought to lie down. I want to call the orderly. But suddenly 1 hear some sort of sound. The sound grows louder. I hear the tramping of feet. And the rattling of canteens. But no shouts. And no shots.

I run out of the dugout. And suddenly a sweet, suffocating wave engulfs me. I shout: "Gas attack!.. Masks!.." And rush into the dugout. My gas mask is hanging there on a nail.

The candle went out when I ran headlong into the dugout. I've found the gas mask with my fingers and begun to put it on. Forgot to open the lower valve. Choke. Opening the valve, I run out into the trenches.

Soldiers are running all around me, wrapping their faces with gauze masks.

After fumbling for matches in my pocket, I light the brushwood lying in front of the trenches. This brushwood was prepared in advance. In case of a gas attack.

Now the flames illuminate our positions. I see that all the grenadiers have come out of the trenches and are lying beside the fires. I also lie down by a fire. I feel bad. My head is spinning. I swallowed a lot of gas when I shouted, "Masks!"

It becomes easier by the fire. Even all right. The flames lift the gas, and it passes over without touching us. I take off my mask.

We lie there for four hours.

It begins to get light. Now you can see the gas moving. It's not a solid wall. It's a cloud of gas ten *sazhens* wide. It slowly advances on us, pushed forward by a soft wind.

We can go to the right or the left – and then the gas will pass by without touching us.

Now it's not frightening. Already I hear laughter and joking somewhere. It's the grenadiers pushing each other into clouds of gas. Guffaws. Horseplay.

I look through the binoculars toward the Germans. Now I see how they release the gas from big bags. It's a repulsive sight. I'm overcome with fury when I see how methodically and coldbloodedly they do it.

I give the order to open fire on these bastards. I give the order to shoot with all the machine guns and rifles, although I realize we'll do little harm – at a distance of fifteen hundred paces.

The grenadiers shoot listlessly. And there aren't many riflemen. Suddenly I see that many of the soldiers are lying dead. They're – the majority. The others are moaning and can't raise themselves from behind the flames.

I hear the sounds of a bugle in the German trenches. It's the poisoners sounding retreat. The gas attack is over.

Leaning on a stick, I blunder to the infirmary. My handkerchief is bloodied from the horrifying vomiting.

I walk down the highway. I see the grass turned yellow and a hundred dead sparrows fallen on the road.

Finale

Our regiment is again off duty.

We're riding on *rozvalni*[2] to the second-class supplies unit: supper will be served there.

The chief of supplies meets his dear guests.

2. Wide and low-slung peasant sleds.

On the table are goatskins of wine, *shashlik* and all sorts of victuals.

I sit at the table with the nurse Klava. I'm already drunk. But I must drink some more. Every glass is accompanied by a toast.

I feel that I shouldn't drink any more. After the gas attack I have disorders of the heart.

In order not to drink, I go out on the street. And sit down on the porch.

Klava comes up and is surprised to find me sitting in the frost without a coat. She takes me by the hand to her room. It's warm there. We sit down on her bed.

But our absence has already been noticed. Laughing and joking, the officers knock on the window of our room.

We go back to the table.

In the morning we return to the regimental station. And I sleep like a log on my army cot.

I wake up from the howling and bursting of bombs. A German plane is bombing the village. This is not the bombardment which we know from the present war. This is four bombs-and the plane leaves.

I go out on the street. Suddenly I feel that I can't breathe. My heart stops. I try to take my pulse; there is no pulse.

With unbelievable difficulty, holding onto the fences, I make it to our location. The physician, shaking his head, shouts:

"Camphor!"

They inject me with camphor.

I lie there, nearly dying. The left side of my chest grows numb. My pulse is forty. "You shouldn't drink," says the physician. "Heart defect."

And I make a vow to myself not to drink anymore.

They transport me to the field hospital through the thawed February snow.

1917-1920

I Don't Understand Anything

The first days of March. I'm riding home from the train station in a buggy.

I ride past the Winter Palace. See a red flag on the palace.

This means a new life. The New Russia. And I am new, not the same as before. Let all that stay behind – my sorrows, nerves, my gloominess, my sick heart.

Ecstatic, I enter my own home. And that very day I make the rounds of all my friends. I see Nadya and her husband. Meet Tata T. Drop in on my university friends.

I see joy and exultation all around. Everyone is glad that the revolution has taken place. Except Nadya, who told me: "It's horrible. It's dangerous for Russia. I don't expect any good to come of it."

For two days I feel splendid. On the third day I have depression again, I have palpitations, gloom and melancholy.

I don't understand anything. I get lost guessing where this despair came from. It simply shouldn't be!

Probably I need to work. Probably I need to give all my strength to the people, the country, the new life.

I go to staff headquarters, to a representative of the Provisional Government. I request that he reassign me to the army.

But I am unfit for the ranks, and they assign me as postmaster to the main post office and telegraph.

A most unpleasant thing for me is done. I sit in an office and sign some papers or other. This work is repellent to me in the extreme.

I go back to headquarters and request a transfer to somewhere in the provinces. They offer me Arkhangelsk – adjutant in the local militia. I accept.

In a week I must leave.

Five O'Clock Tea

The jurist L. stops by to see me. We're getting ready to go to a very aristocratic house – to visit Princess B.

L. asks me to put on my medals.

"She'll like it," he says. "Her husband is still at the front. He commands a division of the guards."

I show him my medals. One medal is on my Caucasian sabre. Two medals are fastened to my cigar box. A fourth medal is worn around the neck. It's awkward somehow for me to put it on. A fifth medal never came into my hands – it's only on paper.

L. insists. He adjusts the medal under the collar of my field jacket.

First published in Russian: 1968
Translation by Gary Kern

Огонь, веревка, пуля и топор

Николай Тихонов

Огонь, веревка, пуля и топор
Как слуги кланялись и шли за нами,
И в каждой капле спал потоп,
Сквозь малый камень прорастали горы,
И в прутике, раздавленном ногою,
Шумели чернорукие леса.

Неправда с нами ела и пила,
Колокола гудели по привычке,
Монеты вес утратили и звон,
И дети не пугались мертвецов...
Тогда впервые выучились мы
Словам прекрасным, горьким и жестоким.

1921

Fire, the rope, the bullet, and the axe
Nikolai Tikhonov

Fire, the rope, the bullet, and the axe –
they bowed to us like servants, followed us,
and torrents slept in every drop of water,
and from each pebble sprang a mountain range,
and every tiny twig crushed underfoot
released the rustling of a black-armed forest.

Lies dined with us and drank with us each night,
bells clanged and clanged simply from force of habit,
coins lost their weight and even lost their ring,
and children weren't frightened of the dead...
Yes, it was then that we first learned by heart
words that are glorious, bitter, and brutal.

1921
Translation by Boris Dralyuk

Въ штыки!..

"Into the fray!"
World War I postcard, Gary Bowman Collection, UNC Chapel Hill

Valentin Katayev volunteered to serve in the Imperial Army in 1915, before he finished high school. He served with distinction, attaining the rank of second lieutenant and receiving two St. George Crosses and an Order of St. Anne for bravery. His frontline experiences made their way into a series of sketches and semi-fictional stories published in Russian newspapers as early as 1915. This story, written much later, sees him returning to his memories of the Great War on the eve of another global conflict.

Near Smorgon
Valentin Katayev

Once, an entire French infantry batallion perished near Verdun. It was following a communications trench, came upon an enemy minefield, and was blown up. Just a few bayonets protruded from the caved-in earth. Later, the French turned this awful mass grave into a monument – filled it with cement and made an inscription. Among wreaths with faded tricolor ribbons, rusted bayonet tips still protrudes from the cement.

Thinking about it, I always recall a different incident, on our Western front in 1916.

Our battery was stationed near Smorgon, to the left of the famous road from Minsk to Vilnius that Napoleon's army followed in its retreat. We all know the road from Vereshyagin's painting: a bitter winter, a striped pole, and a row of mourning birches. But when we were there it was spring, the end of a fresh Belorussian May. From our battery we could see the long line of Kutuzov's birches, grown much taller and thicker in a hundred years. They were ripped and splintered in a few places by enemy shells, but we enjoyed their bright appearance, and the freshness of their new foliage.

There had been a lull for the second week running. Taking advantage of it, we had done a great job camoflaging our artillery with young pine branches, digging and paving walkways, setting up little benches and tables by the dugouts, and drawing chess boards on them – in all, we turned our battery into a lovely little place. Then we took baths, sewed buttons, fixed up our weapons; picked some grass and gave our canisters and bowls a good scrub; and then, finally, we got juniper-branch fires going, hung up some buckets, and all boiled our laundry, the whole troop together. Once it was all boiled and wrung dry, we didn't hang it up right away, so that the enemy's air recon wouldn't spot our battery. We knew better than to do that. We waited patiently for the last enemy plane, surrounded by leaping scraps of shrapnel, to disappear deep into enemy lines. We knew perfectly well that no more enemy airplanes would fly that day. So we went ahead and threw our white shirts and drawers all over the pine-branch camoflage. Waiting for the laundry to dry, everyone in the battery went to relax and have fun.

The phone operators, all together, went off into the field to play *gorodki*, or "skrakli," the name we picked up from the Poles.

Cannonier Vlasov, an elderly, osprey-looking soldier with flaxen hair, and the only one in the battery to own a razor, had set up a barber shop by his dugout and was already using a cold swab to lather up the tough chin of his platoon leader, senior gunner Bondarchuk, strict in service, but vain in daily life, a man who liked to be served.

The short-legged scout Vorona, who had come over from the scouts' team in the first-class supply train to see his countryman Prokosha Kolykhaev, was dancing to a balalaika and walking on his hands, surrounded by a silent audience.

Samsonov, a blue-eyed young volunteer with a St. George cross, dragging his overcoat by the sleeve, was heading off to the birches to read Fyodor Sologub's novel *The Petty Demon*.

The beast-like but childishly kind Siberian Gorbunov, who had just recently learned to write, was writing a letter – terribly slowly, huffing and puffing, reading each word syllable by syllable – to Tobolsk, to his dear wife Varvara Denisovna. His gap-toothed mouth was colored violet from his copying pencil.

Hunching his sweaty shoulders under cloth epaulettes, Gorbunov labored over the corner of a thin-legged table, the rest of which was taken up by two artillery gunners – 5th and 6th gun – playing cards with a silent intensity.

Only warrant officer Chigrinsky, a knight of all four classes of the Order of St. George, considered participation in soldiers' pasttimes to be below him, even though he really wanted to. He had just come over to the battery from his private dugout, set up between the battery and the officers' quarters.

Chigrinsky, pretending to be pensive, strolled along the line of guns, frowning and using the edge of his saffron-scented hand to even out his old-fashioned moustache, waxed and black with a hint of grey. But boredom was getting the best of him. He couldn't maintain his estrangement. With his arms folded behind him like a general, his stomach jutting out a bit with its nice, ringed officer's belt, he stopped by the third gun, where the group of people most deserving of his presence had gathered: several gun layers, two platoon leaders, three artillery commanders, and the battery's sentry, junior gunner Lepko, a joker and a merry fellow.

Lepko was telling jokes. Catching sight of the warrant officer, he cut himself off mid-sentence, jumped down from the turf-covered dugout roof, clicked his spurs together, and touched his hand to the visor of his bent-back cap.

"Telling jokes?" Chigrinsky asked, with a condescending sneer.

"Sir, yes, sir!" Lepko reported.

"You're the one telling?"

"Yes, sir, I am!"

"All right, then, no need to stand. Sit on down and continue. As for me, I'll set myself up here somewhere, and listen to your nonsense for a bit."

The soldiers moved aside, and respectfully offered a seat to their superior.

"So what's your joke about?" the officer asked, rearranging his tunic made of the highest-quality cloth.

"His joke, Kapiton Ivanovich," answered blacksmith and gunner Ulier, a Bessarabian gypsy with a giant blue beard, in his sing-song voice, "his joke is about how he ended up in heaven."

"I haven't heard that one before. I'll listen. Lepko, report. From the beginning."

Lepko's hazel eyes twinkled, and he winked mischievously at his listeners.

"Sir, I'll just need your word that you won't be offended or hold anything against me later."

"Why's that?"

"Because in that there joke, there's a bit about you, sir. It's just the joke, is all."

"All right. That's fine. I'll allow it."

Lepko jumped up onto the roof of the dugout, placed his sabre between his legs, cocked his cap still further back, licked his lips, and began telling in a sharp, girly voice, from up where he was down into the trench.

"So it was, one time, my turn to go stand guard at the lookout, and while I'm out there, suddenly an enemy shell comes flying down, and in a split second that enemy shell knocks me dead, right where I stand. So I'm dead where I stand, and in that same second two angels grab me by the arms, carry me up to the sky, and put me right in front of the gates of heaven. Naturally, out comes apostle Peter, and asks: 'What's all this noise? Who's there?' I tell him: 'Sir, junior gunner Lepko of the 64th artillery brigade, 1st battery, killed this same day while standing guard, reporting to heaven, sir.' He looks me over from all sides and says: 'Go on back, we don't take hicks like you into heaven.' 'What d'you mean, hicks? Don't take 'em? How's that possible? That's new! You have no right! When I was enlisting for active duty, the priest said: any soldier who serves with care, has respect for his direct superior, and then dies in honorable combat for faith, for the tsar, and for the fatherland – that soldier will most definitely be taken right to you and into heaven. What kind of issue can there be?' But he still doesn't want to let me through, and says: 'This isn't my decision. I'm going to report this to the Lord, and it'll be whatever He decides.' Okay. So apostle Peter goes to God, comes back, and says: 'All right, you're allowed. The Lord says that any soldier who performs his active service with care, has respect for his direct superior, and then dies in honorable combat for faith, for the tsar, and for the fatherland – that soldier will most definitely be taken right to us and into heaven. C'mon in, you little twerp! Just wipe your boots, we keep things clean in here.' So I wiped my boots on the grass and went into heaven. Well, obviously, we all know what heaven's like: clean, no doubt about it. No filth under your feet. What's under your feet is actually the blue sky, which, if you look up from here on the battery, is then above. And from there, going the other way, it's below. Just how it is."

With that, Lepko looked up. Everyone followed suit, looking up pensively. The May sky's blue dome covered the earth. The sun was setting behind enemy lines. Fiery dust hung in the air. And through that blinding dust a light mass was visible just on the horizon – the fishbone-shaped ruins of the Smorgon church.

Oh, May evening by the woods, how faithfully my memory has kept you!

"So here I am, walking around heaven," Lepko continued, glancing slyly at the warrant officer. "Just walking around for an hour, then two, then three. Various see-through angels are wandering around me. That's all fine. But then all of a sudden I get awfully hungry. Nothing to laugh about! What's so surprising about that? Since death I hadn't had a single bite. Then I see: there goes one of their archangels with a fiery sword – probably the sentry for heaven – either Gabriel, or maybe Michael, I don't know."

"If he's with a sword, must be Michael," came the sing-song voice of Ulier the gypsy.

"Fine, let him be Michael. So I say to him: 'Listen, d'you give out any rations around here? 'Cause I'm pretty hungry.' And he says to me: 'No, no, of course not! You're such an ignorant soldier! This is heaven, not earth, and no one eats, because – can't you see? – the only things here are disembodied souls, meaning see-through ones.' 'Well I don't know about no disembodied souls. Could be. But me, personally, I gotta eat. Right now.' 'That's not allowed.' 'What d'you mean, "not allowed"? Can't be. Take me to the Lord.' 'Okay.' Off we go to see their God. Of course, we all know what God looks like: he's sitting on this kind of throne thing, with pastures all around. 'What's this ruckus?' He asks, 'What's the issue?' I say to Him: 'So here's the deal, they won't let me eat, what's with that?' And that Michael or Gabriel or whatever, he reports: 'This is that same junior gunner Lepko, 64th artillery brigade, 1st battery, who died in honorable combat for faith, for the tsar, and for the fatherland.' God asks: 'Good soldier?' I answer: 'Of course! I served according to all regulations, always had respect for my immediate superiors. Even the warrant officer can confirm. And if you don't give me any food, then I'd rather leave your heaven – the devil with this whole thing!' God thought for a spell, and then says: 'If you're a good soldier, served according to regulations, had respect for your immediate superior, and died for faith, for the tsar, and for the fatherland in honorable combat, then we have no choice. Give him something to eat.' So they gave me a full canister of fried meat, half a loaf of white bread, and a cypress-wood spoon.

"I went off to the side, sat under some heavenly bush, and had a proper lunch, and then went to sleep. As soon as I lie down to sleep, that Michael or Gabriel guy wakes me up: 'Hey, soldier! Get up! Sleeping is not allowed in heaven. In heaven we only have disembodied souls. They never sleep.' 'Aw, to hell with all of you! Take me to God.' We go back to God. 'What's this ruckus?' He says, 'What's the issue?' 'The soldier wants to sleep!..'

Lepko recounted about how God thought for a bit and let him sleep. Then, how when he woke up, Lepko wanted a smoke, and how the archangel didn't allow it, and how they went to God, and how God, again, thought for a bit and ordered they give him an eighth of an ounce of Troika tobacco, a copy of the newspaper *Russian Word*, and two boxes of new-style matches. "Let him smoke, so that his family doesn't complain."

Lepko told his story with great care and detail, without rushing, at times spitting off to the side and twirling a beet-colored revolver ribbon on his chest.

Chigrinsky wouldn't stop frowning.

"So where's the part about me?" he finally asked, with apparent nonchalance. "I'm not noticing it."

"It's coming up, Kapiton Ivanovich," Lepko said quickly. "This here is a pretty long joke, a good hour and a half. So anyway, I rolled up and smoked two cigarettes out of the Troika and the *Russian Word*, and then I realize that I really need to go. I go running around heaven to find the right place for that sort of thing. I run and run, but I don't see anything appropriate. So what should I do? That's when that Michael-Gabriel comes up to me: 'Why are you running about, soldier?' 'I gotta, y'know, go.' He actually got mad: 'Are you crazy? This is heaven, not God knows what!' I'm nearly crying here: 'Take me to God, quick.' We go. 'What's this ruckus?' The archangel reports: here's the deal. God thinks a bit and says: 'It's not allowed.' "'Not allowed?'" I yell. 'How can it be not allowed when I can't hold it in anymore?! Seriously, what's with this? You let me eat, but won't let me go! Then just send me back to my troop!' God, in return, thinks some more and says: 'Since he's a good soldier and suffered for faith, for the tsar, and for the fatherland in honorable combat, then, given that we did, in fact, give him food, we have no choice. It's allowed. Just take him off to the side.' So the archangel takes me about 100 steps away, picks a quiet spot behind some heavenly trees, takes out his fiery sword, and cuts a clean little circle in the sky. The sky up there, it's, y'know, blue and hard, like it's glass, or more like porcelain. 'Go 'head,' he says. I look down at the earth, and reply: 'Listen, you'll have to excuse me, but I can't do it here. Cut me a circle somewhere else.' 'Why's that?' 'Here, look.' The archangel looks down: and down there, right under us, was our battery, and in it, a bench, and on that bench was you, Kapiton Ivanovich. 'See?' I ask the archangel. 'Sure,' he says. 'What of it?' 'I couldn't possibly treat my warrant officer like that. He always liked me, he never sent me out on tour out of order, and he said he'll definitely let me off next week, so I can go home.' And that Gabriel-Michael guy, he just waves me away and goes: 'Naw, go 'head. Don't worry. He's not going to let you off. He's just leading you on.'

And the moment Lepko got to the last word of his long tale, the air jerked, and four explosions – four black columns of earth – rose slowly in front of the battery.

Tripping, falling, and grabbing laundry as they ran, everyone in the battery rushed to the dugouts.

Four artillery shots sounded weakly in the distance, and almost at once four new eight-inch shells stormed down, landing behind and covering the battery in a downpour of black earth.

The next four shells exploded right on our line. Splinters, pieces of sod, pine branches, buckets, shirts – everything flew into the air. But we were already perched on our bunks in the dugouts, listening in terror to the piercing whistle of enemy shells wreaking havoc above. The walls wobbled and shifted. Rivulets of dry dust ran down them. Pieces of earth covered up the tiny windows. A greenish, stifling darkness filled the dugouts. We remained silent, subdued. We were afraid to glance at each other, even to budge. We thought that the slightest movement could bring instantaneous death. At the same time we knew what had happened. A simple thing, really.

We had been wary of enemy planes, but had completely forgotten about their gas balloons. One such "sausage," set up by the enemy beyond Smorgon and invisible in the sunset's fiery dust, had discovered our laundry-covered battery.

I know of no power in the world that could save us!

More than forty minutes, with perfect aim, the enemy's battery of eight-inch guns literally destroyed us, with superhuman, brutal, methodical precision.

Several hundred 400-pound shells turned our battery – our lovely little place with its chess tables, benches, flower beds, and walkways – into a completely black, wavy, plowed field.

In the funereal gloom of the dugout it seemed as though several days had passed.

And then, by the time we were convinced that this hell would never end, there suddenly came a complete, profound, blessed, angelic silence. We waited five minutes, ten, and finally, carefully, one by one, started to emerge from the earth.

The sharp orange stripe of sunset floated before our gaze.

We were almost completely deaf. The world around floated in an unbearable silence. But then the sounds started to come back. A May bug flew by with a thick buzz.

A fresh breeze carried away the stench of burnt stockade, wafting up from the hot craters over the battery. In came the strong, cool, refreshing smell of foliage and pine needles. We started to review our casualties, but it turned out there were none. Not only were there none dead or injured, no one was even concussed. Just a few had been deafened, but they were coming to. Not a single shell had hit an occupied dugout, or a piece of artillery. Two shells had hit the telephone operators' dugout, but it was empty: the operators, who had been playing "skrakli" far out in the field, hadn't had time to reach their dugout, and had found shelter in another. The operators' dugout was completely destroyed, but on one of the broken ceiling beams, untouched by explosions as if by some miracle, hung a kerosene lamp with its round tin lampshade – the pride of the rich and independent operators.

For a good while we didn't know what do, and sat uncertainly on the ground, using our sleeves to wipe off our sweaty, black-nosed and black-eared faces.

Suddenly the battery sentry, junior gunner Lepko, leaped up, fixed his cap, turned around, and yelled:

"All rise, atten-shun!"

He had noticed our brigade's commander, Major General Aleshin, who was walking across the mangled earth toward our battery with his aide. The general had left his automobile on the road. From there, the battery must have looked completely wiped out. His face was whiter than a sheet, his lips were trembling. He would stumble, at times appearing to sink up to his chest into the ground, at times rising to the top of a mound of dirt, so that we could see the very tips of his chrome boots with their tiny spurs.

When he had come close enough, junior gunner Lepko, his hand in a salute, took off towards him, froze four steps away, knocked his big bronze spurs together, cupped his left hand to gesture backward, jutted out his chest as much as he pulled in his stomach, and in a debonair, brisk, girly voice cried out loud enough for the echo to bounce back from the far-off woods:

"Your Excellency! First battery of your 64th brigade! Sentry for the battery, junior gunner Lepko, reporting! No incidents during my watch, sir!"

And he jumped aside to let the general through.

The general started to greet us, saluted, cut off, looked at us – black and terrifying as we were – and suddenly, tears began to stream down his aged white face. He waved us aside and, stumbling as he went, walked back, and his aide, sub-lieutenant Shreder, followed suit, stooping and wobbling on his lanky dragoon legs.

As for us, we started digging out the guns.

First published in Russian: 1939
Translation by Eugenia Sokolskaya

Give the Gift of Chtenia

If you love Chtenia, why not share it with family and friends?

Chtenia is the world's only regularly published journal of Russian readings in translation. Each quarterly issue contains 128+ pages of quality translations of literature, memoirs, poetry, plays and miscellany (alongside fine black and white photography), all gathered together about a selected theme, like Childhood, Dacha life, Hope, Spring, Love or Luck.

To start your gift subscription, just complete and mail in the subscription form below... We'll send your recipient a gift card notice and begin their subscription with the most current issue.

❏ **YES!** Please start a gift subscription to *Chtenia* for the person indicated below. Please find enclosed payment of $35 ($43 outside the US) by:

❏ Check ❏ Amex ❏ Visa ❏ Mastercard ❏ Discover

Credit card no.: _____

Expire date: _____ Signature: _____

BILL SUBSCRIPTION TO:

Name _____

Address _____

_____

City _____ State _____ Zip _____

Country _____

MAIL SUBSCRIPTION TO:

Name _____

Address _____

_____

City _____ State _____ Zip _____

Country _____

Complete and mail to:
RIS Publications, PO Box 567, Montpelier, VT 05601

Мама и убитый немцами вечер

Владимир Маяковский

По черным улицам белые матери
судорожно простерлись, как по гробу глазет.
Вплакались в орущих о побитом неприятеле:
«Ах, закройте, закройте глаза газет!»

Письмо.

Мама, громче!
Дым.
Дым.
Дым еще!

Что вы мямлите, мама, мне?
Видите —
весь воздух вымощен
громыхающим под ядрами камнем!
Ма - а - а - ма!
Сейчас притащили израненный вечер.
Крепился долго,
кургузый,
шершавый,
и вдруг, —
надломивши тучные плечи,
расплакался, бедный, на шее Варшавы.
Звезды в платочках из синего ситца
визжали:
«Убит,
дорогой,
дорогой мой!»
И глаз новолуния страшно косится
на мертвый кулак с зажатой обоймой.
Сбежались смотреть литовские села,
как, поцелуем в обрубок вкована,
слезя золотые глаза костелов,
пальцы улиц ломала Ковна.
А вечер кричит,
безногий,
безрукий,
«Неправда,
я еще могу-с —
хе! —
выбряцав шпоры в горящей мазурке,
выкрутить русый ус!»

Звонок.

Что вы,
мама?
Белая, белая, как на гробе глазет.
"Оставьте!
О нем это,
об убитом, телеграмма.
Ах, закройте,
закройте глаза газет!”

Mama and the Evening Killed by the Germans
Vladimir Mayakovsky

Along the black streets, white mothers
spasmodically spread, like brocade on a coffin.
They wept their way into the crowd shouting about the beaten enemy:
"Ach, shut their eyes, shut the newspapers' eyes!"

A letter.

Mama, louder!
Smoke.
Smoke.
More smoke!
What's that you're mumbling, Mama, to me?
Don't you see —
The air is paved
with stone rumbling under artillery fire!
Ma-a-a-ma!
They just brought in an evening all covered in wounds.
He held on for a long time,
spread too tight,
rough around the edges,
and suddenly —
his cloud shoulders broke down;
he burst into tears, the poor guy, on Warsaw's breast.
The stars, on their hankies of dark-blue cotton,
screeched out:
"He's killed,
my dear,
my dear one!"
And the new moon's eye squinted terribly
at the dead fist clenching a cartridge clip.
Lithuanian villages gathered round to watch,
as Kaunas, forged by a kiss into one giant stump,
bringing tears to the golden eyes of its churches,
wrung its street-fingered hands.
But the evening cried out,
legless,
armless:
"You've got it all wrong,
I'm still quite able —
ha! —
clanging my spurs in a burning mazurka,
to twirl my golden-brown mustache!"

The doorbell.

What's wrong,
Mama?
White, white as brocade on a coffin.
"Leave me alone!
It's about him,
he's been killed — a telegram.
Ach, shut their eyes,
shut the newspapers' eyes!"

First published in Russian: 1914
Translation by James H. McGavran III

"A Typical Group of Cossacks"
Capt. Donald C. Thompson (1917)

At the symbolic level, one of Ivan Bunin's most celebrated short stories, "The Gentleman from San Francisco" (1915), dramatizes the collapse of a system of values that had seemed indomitable a short while before. It was quite clearly a reaction to the cataclysm of the Great War, then unfolding before the author's eyes. "The Cold Fall," written many years later in the nostalgic vein of his émigré fiction (and with a female narrator), addresses the direct effects of this cataclysm on a single human life.

The Cold Fall
Ivan Bunin

In June of that year he was a guest at our estate. He always had been like one of the family; his late father was a friend and neighbor of my father. On June 15 Francis Ferdinand was killed in Sarajevo. They delivered the newspapers from the post office on the morning of the sixteenth. Holding the Moscow evening paper, Father came out of his study into the dining room, where he, Mother, and I were still drinking tea, and said, "Well, my friends, it's war! They've killed the Austrian archduke at Sarajevo. That means war!"

On Saint Peter's Day we had a number of guests – for Father's name day – and at the dinner table our engagement was announced. But on July 19 Germany declared war on Russia.

He came in September but stayed only a day and night – to say good-bye before his departure for the front (at that time everyone thought the war would end soon; our marriage was postponed until spring). And so we were spending our last evening together. After supper, as was customary, they brought in the samovar, and looking at the windows, all misted over with its steam, Father said, "An incredibly early and cold fall!"

We sat quietly that evening, merely exchanging meaningless words from time to time, exaggeratedly calm, concealing our secret thoughts and feelings. Even Father's remark about the autumn was full of feigned non-chalance. I walked up to the door of the terrace and wiped the glass with a handkerchief; out in the garden clear, icy stars were glittering brightly and distinctly in the black sky.

Leaning back in his easy chair, Father smoked, gazing vacantly at the hot lamp hanging over the table; Mother sat under its light in her spectacles, carefully stitching together a small silk pouch. We understood its purpose – and felt both touched and frightened. Father said, "So you want to go early in the morning all the same, and not after lunch?"

"Yes, with your permission, in the morning," he answered. "Sad to say, I still have things to get arranged at home."

Father let out a brief sigh.

"All right, my dear boy, whatever you think. But in that case it's time for Mama and me to get some sleep; we don't want to miss seeing you off tomorrow."

Mother stood up and made the sign of the cross over her future son; he bent to kiss her hand, then Father's. Left alone, we stayed for a time in the dining room – for some reason I decided to lay out a game of solitaire. He paced silently from corner to corner, then asked, "Want to take a little walk?"

Feeling more downhearted than ever, I responded impassively, "All right."

Still in a pensive mood as he found his coat in the anteroom, he recalled Fet's verses with a sweet, wry smile: "The autumn's so frosty this year! / Put on your capote and your shawl. . ."

"I don't have a capote. How does it go after that?"

"Can't remember. Like this, I think: 'Look there, in the pine wood, my dear; / It's a fire, so it seems, rising tall.'"

"What kind of fire?"

"The rising moon, of course. There's a sort of rural autumn charm in those lines: 'Put on your capote and your shawl.' The days of our grandfathers and grandmothers... Oh God, my God!"

"What's wrong?"

"Nothing, dear. It's sad, all the same. Sad and good. I love you so very much."

When we had put on our coats we went through the dining room, onto the terrace, then down into the garden. At first it was so dark that I had to hold on to his sleeve. Then the ever brighter sky began revealing black branches strewn with the mineral glitter of stars. Pausing for a moment, he turned toward the manor house.

"Look how the windows of the house are shining in some absolutely special way, in an autumn way. I'll remember this evening as long as I live, forever."

I turned to look, and he embraced me in my Swiss wrap. I pushed aside the downy kerchief from my face and let my head fall back so he could kiss me. After we had kissed he looked in my face.

"How your eyes are gleaming," he said. "Aren't you cold? The air is just like winter. All the same, if I'm killed, you won't forget me right away?"

I thought, "And what if he is killed? Could I really forget him in a short time – for isn't everything forgotten in the end?" Frightened by my thoughts, I answered hurriedly, "Don't say that! I could never go on living without you!"

After a brief silence he said slowly, "Well then, if I'm killed, I'll wait for you there. You just live, enjoy your life on earth, then come to me."

I burst into bitter tears.

In the morning he left. Mama hung around his neck the ominous little pouch that she had sewn the previous evening – it contained a golden icon worn by her father and grandfather in time of war – and in a paroxysm of desperation we made the sign of the cross over him. Watching as he rode away, we stood on the porch in that state of torpor that one always experiences when seeing off someone for a long separation, feeling only the amazing incongruity between us and the joyous sunny morning all around, with its glistening rime frost on the grass. We stood there awhile, then went back into the emptiness of the house. I walked through the rooms, hands behind my back, not knowing what to do with myself, whether to start sobbing or to sing out as loud as I could.

He was killed – what a strange word! – a month later, in Galicia. Thirty whole years have passed since then. And I have lived through so very much during those years, which seem to have lasted for ages when you think about them attentively, when you turn over in memory all that magical, inscrutable something, a mystery to both mind and heart, that is called the past. In the spring of 1918, after Father and Mother had both died, I was living in Moscow, in the cellar of a trader-woman from the Smolensk market who always used to mock me: "Well, now, Your Excellency, how's your life expectancy?" I too was engaged in huckstering. As so many others were doing at that time, I was selling what few things I still possessed to soldiers in Caucasian fur hats and unbuttoned greatcoats – some sort of ring, or a small cross, or a moth-eaten fur collar. And there, selling things on the corner of Arbat and the market, I met a rare, beautiful person, an elderly retired military man, whom I soon married and with whom I went away in April to Yekaterinodar. It took us nearly two weeks to get there. We traveled with his nephew, a boy of about seventeen, who was working his way south to join the volunteer forces. I went as a peasant woman in bast sandals; my husband wore a tattered Cossack smock and let his black and gray-streaked beard grow out. We remained in the Don and Kuban regions for more than two years. In a winter storm we sailed with a huge mob of other refugees from Novorossisk to Turkey, and during the voyage, at sea, my husband died of typhus. After that I had only three relations left on all the earth: my husband's nephew, his young wife, and their daughter, a baby of seven months. But soon the nephew and wife sailed away to the Crimea to join Wrangel's forces, leaving the baby in my hands. There they disappeared without a trace. After that I stayed on for a long time in Constantinople, earning a living for myself and the child by the most burdensome manual labor. Then, as did so many others, she and I began wandering here, there, and everywhere: Bulgaria, Serbia, Czechoslovakia, Belgium, Paris, Nice... Long since grown, the girl remained in Paris, became altogether French, quite comely, and absolutely indifferent to me. She worked in a chocolate shop near the Madeleine; her sleek hands with the silver nails wrapped boxes in satiny paper and tied them up with thin, golden twine. And I lived and still live in Nice on whatever the Lord happens to send me... I had first been to Nice in 1912 – and in those happy times I never could have imagined what it would become for me someday!

So I went on living after his death, having once rashly sworn that if he died I could never go on. But in recalling everything that I have lived through since then, I always ask myself, "What, after all, does my life consist of?" And I answer, "Only of that cold fall evening." Was there ever really such an evening? Yes, all the same, there was. And that's all there ever was in my life – the rest is a useless dream. And I believe, I fervently believe that somewhere out there he's waiting for me – with the very same love and youthfulness as on that evening. "You just live, enjoy your life on earth, then come to me..." Well, I've lived, I've had my joy; now I'll be coming soon.

May 3, 1944
Translation by Robert Bowie